when he's DIRTY

NEW YORK TIMES BESTSELLING AUTHOR
LISA RENEE JONES

ISBN-13: 979-8552322275

Dear Reader

Thank you so much for joining me for yet another Walker Security adventure (and if it's your first time in this world, I hope you love it enough to check out the other series connected to these swoonworthy alphas). It's hard to believe that Tall, Dark, and Deadly is now eight years old! These characters are close to my heart and I hope they are close to yours as well. Please note that I do occasionally take some liberties and in this series, the District Attorney becomes the first elected DA in Texas. In Texas, the DA is actually appointed by the Governor. I always like to share those notes. I hope you are all warm, safe, and healthy. These are crazy times and I appreciate you escaping reality with me! Speaking of Escaping Reality, The Secret Life of Amy Bensen is coming to Passionflix next year. Stay tuned!

Much love and appreciation to my loyal readers!

xoxo,
Lisa

2

Chapter One

ADRIAN

Every Friday night, anyone on the Walker Security team that isn't covered in blood, or trying to keep someone else from being covered in blood, gets together and decompresses. New York City weather permitting, as of late, which means tag football. And tag football with these guys is a good way to get tackled and in a fight. Which is why I play—it's why we all play. Well, that and the food and beer after the brawls.

Adam, an ex-SEAL who was on the elite Team Six but is too freaking humble to talk about it, is—fittingly—our quarterback. He's tall, powerful, agile, and smart. He's also a good guy, better than me, but I saved the fucker's life, so he thinks that makes me a good guy too. He's wrong.

He throws wide and left and I'm wide and left. I leap in the air, snag the ball, and Lucas, nicknamed Lucifer, the newest member of Walker, takes me down hard. "Ouch," he whispers in my ear. "I think that hurt."

I curse at him in Spanish, and ironically, my white father would be proud, my Latina mama, not so much. He chuckles and stands up, offering me his hand. He's blond, muscled, tatted up, and tall as fuck, considering I'm six-one and he's looking down at me. I don't know his story beyond him being our newest pilot, willing to fly high-risk, big payday missions. All I know is that his nickname bugs the *fuck* out of me for good reason—it hits a nerve. Still, I take his hand and stand up, holding up the ball for all to see.

Rick Savage snatches it from my hand. "To think I used to hate your ass." He winks—a trained assassin with a scar down his cheek who acts like a goofball—right up until the moment he kills you. Maybe even in that moment.

"Now you're all kinds of cute," he adds.

I wiggle my eyebrows. "Should we talk to your wife?"

"Sorry, man, not happening. We keep this between us. She's still prettier than you." He jogs away and I laugh, which says a lot where Savage and I are concerned. Right out of the gate, we were oil and water, hate to friendship, wash, and repeat several times over until we landed at friendship. After two years, I get him now. He doesn't get me, though. He just thinks he does. Scrubbing grass from my goatee and then running a hand over my thick, dark hair, I line up for another play, eyeing Lucifer and pointing at him, telling him I'm coming for him. Two more plays in, we've switched sides of the ball and I take his ass down.

"Ouch," I whisper at his ear. "I think that hurt."

Lucifer gives an evil laugh and says, "Pain is the sweet stuff, man. Oh so sweet."

I decide right then he's as evil as his laugh. I might end up liking him after all.

The game ends and we all end up at Asher's house, another blond, tatted-up dude who was on SEAL Team Six with Adam. Asher's a good guy, married, stable, and nifty as hell at hacking. I'm in the kitchen at the island drinking a beer with him and Adam, while Adam talks about some asshole who tried to mug a woman in the subway this morning. Of course, Adam handled it. This is usually where I'd tell some stupid joke, about him liking the purse more than the other guy, a time when I'd fit in, and seem like less of an asshole than I am, but today I'm not that guy. I thought the game and the guys were just what I needed to get my mind off my problem. I mean, I do like the Walker team and pretty much everyone here. This a brotherhood, a place where you belong when you belong nowhere else. But today I question if being with them was ever a smart choice.

My cellphone buzzes and the sound rattles my normally unshakable nerves, for the very reason I'm doubting my place here. It's all about my life before Walker that just won't let me go.

I snake my phone from my pocket, glace at the number that means bad news, and send it to voicemail, at least for now. I eye Asher who's talking about all but getting his ass kicked on a job mission. "Obviously, you Team Sixers don't know how to fight the Mexican way."

Asher arches a brow. "Which is how?"

"Dirty. I'd explain what that means, but I'd have to kill you."

Savage appears at the end of the island and smirks. "Your pops is white. You told me so. In other words, you fight just like us white guys."

"You never saw my mama when she was pissed off," I assure him. "My mama would have made you her little bitch, Savage."

Savage smirks. "You're the little bitch."

"When my mama got a hold of me, yeah. I was."

Everyone laughs and my phone starts ringing again, and thanks to Savage running his mouth, I easily slip away from the group.

I walk away, feeling all kinds of dirty, and not because I'm Mexican. I'm proud of my heritage. I loved my mother dearly and so did my father. Even so, despite inheriting her dark hair and brown eyes, no one thinks I'm Mexican. It works for me, it means I can play the Latin role or not, I'm easy that way. And that's exactly how I ended up undercover for the Feds on the case that pretty much gutted my life. I was seasoned, a good choice for a dangerous job. And the devil incarnate, our target, liked me. More and more, I'm not sure if that's a testament to my skills or my character.

"Someone else is dead," I say, skipping the niceties, which my caller will understand. Kirk Pitt was on the same task force I was when we took on the King Devil, Nick Waters—the leader of one of the most notorious biker gangs in the world. He just wasn't on the inside of the club like I was. He wasn't ruined like I was.

"Yes," he confirms. "Another one down. We need you, man, or Waters is going to get off. The ADA on this case is asking for you."

My lips thin. We got Waters and a shit ton of his people on everything from extortion to murder to sex trafficking. The problem is I'm one of the only credible witnesses that can pull all the pieces together.

"I bet she is," I say.

"She's legit, man."

"And you know that how?"

"Her reputation."

"You forget that nothing gets Nick Waters off like turning a good girl going bad."

"All those years you were under were for nothing if he's the one getting off."

"Which is exactly what happens if I'm dead," I say.

"Adrian, man—"

"What does she know about me?"

"She knows you by your real name, Adrian Mack, not Adrian Ramos. Your photos and file remain top secret to protect your identity but she's read your written testimony."

"What about John Jacobs?" I ask. "He's the CEO of a the next best thing to Facebook. He was Waters' partner. Where are you on getting him to roll over on Waters?"

"Nowhere. He's not even in the picture. He knows we don't have shit on him. He and Waters will be back in business in no time without you. Call the prosecutor, man. Talk to her."

My lips thin. "Text me her information. I'll think about it."

"I'll text you right fucking now because you don't have a lot of time on this, none of us do. The trial is only six weeks away. He knows you're out there. He knows you can come for him. You think he's not coming for you?"

A muscle in my jaw ticks. "I'll be in touch."

I disconnect and my phone immediately buzzes with a text message. I sit down on a living room chair and click the Dropbox link Kirk just sent me. The first document is a photo of a gorgeous brunette with blue eyes. Priscilla Miller, often called "Pri," spent years working for her father's high-profile law firm, helping bad guys walk free. She did well. She made a lot of money. Then one day, she quit and joined the good guys at the district attorney's office, walked away from the money in the process. Only, things like that don't just happen. I know. I didn't just randomly wake up and decide to leave the Feds. Shit happened. I had motivation. I want to know what motivated Pri. I have to know. Because this woman is now more a part of my past and my future than any other woman ever has been in my lifetime. Some might say she could be the life or death of me. I'd say I'm the life or death of her.

If she's dirty, I might just have to kill her. If she's not, I have to keep her alive.

Chapter Two

ADRIAN

I glance up from the electronic file I'm looking at to find Asher and Savage's wives hugging all over them. Fuck. Fuck. Fuck. They're family men now, and once a Walker becomes a family man, he backs out of the more dangerous jobs. They've had their big paydays. They've done their time. They stay home and safe. They keep their wives safe.

I'm putting them in danger just being here.

I *can't* be here, not until this is over. Maybe not ever again.

Pushing to my feet, I head for the door and I don't look back. Exiting the apartment, I wait until I'm in the elevator and punch in a text to Raf, my younger brother by six years, and the only family I have left: *I'm hot right now. That means you are, too. Keep your security tight. I'll call you later.*

Thank fuck being an international pop star means he has security, and as a bonus, he's not on tour right now. He replies instantly: *Stay alive, damn it.*

I've prepared him for this. He knows what's going on. He knows a lot of things I wish he didn't have to know.

The elevator dings and I waste no time exiting the building, stepping outside and cutting right, only to hear, "Adrian."

I stop dead at Blake Walker's voice, cursing under my breath. Blake is one of the three Walker brothers, the youngest, and the one who brought me into Walker. A world-class hacker, perhaps the best in the world, I suspect he knows more about me than even Adam, who introduced us. I rotate to find him leaning on the wall, booted feet crossed, his long dark hair now shoulder-length, and wild from the wicked wind that blew in an hour ago, with the promise of a hurricane. "Where the fuck do you think you're going?" he demands, pushing off the wall.

"You know," I say, because of course, *he knows*.

"I do know," he says. "And I also know your ass should be hunting me down to help. But you weren't, were you?"

"The farther I am from the team, the safer they are."

He laughs. "Come on, man. We're the guys who stand when everyone else falls. You know that. You're one of us."

"He'll come after the people I care about. He'll come after you and your wife."

"You know my wife," he says. "She'd love the chance to be the one to castrate him." He narrows his intelligent eyes on me. Blake sees too much. All the fucking time. "He wants you to come to him. He's waiting for you."

"I know," I say. "And I'm sure as fuck not going to disappoint him. I'm not waiting for someone else to die. Anyone and everyone linked to this case are in danger."

"Agreed. We need to save them and get you on the stand, testifying against this dickhead." The doors to the building open and Lucifer and Adam step outside and fuck me, they each take a spot on either side of me. "This is your team." Blake hands me a leather bag from over his shoulder. "And this is a rundown of everyone attached to the case. I started hacking the minute the first body dropped."

I don't reach for the bag. I'm blown away by Blake staying this in tune with the case, but then, I am a danger to the team. He knew there was a risk.

"Do you know the irony of sending me to take down the King Devil with Adam and Lucifer?"

He grins. "Fuck yeah, I do. And I love it. Flights are grounded. I got you clearance. Lucifer is flying you out, off the radar, and he'll be with you to get you out fast if needed. Adam is a master of disguises. You need him on this one."

"You're going to get them killed."

"I'm going to keep your stubborn ass alive," he counters. "You three are going to keep everyone else alive. Smith and Wes are going to keep your brother alive. They're already at the airport. Make sure Raf knows they're coming."

"You sent Smith and Wes to protect my brother?"

"Fuck yes," Blake says. "He might have good security, but he didn't have us. Now, he does."

He's right. Raf needs protection and Walker is ten levels above anyone else. And I'm now torn in two directions. I don't want to take Walker down with me, but they're not going to let me go at this alone. But I also can't walk away from this. Not after the two years I spent with the King Devil, as Waters called himself, sinning right alongside him. "I should have killed him."

"Never let the devil steal your soul," Blake warns.

I don't reply, but Nick Waters did that and more.

"There's a vehicle at the curb waiting for you," Blake says. "Now go, all of you, before you can't get off the ground for the hellish wind. And stay the fuck alive. That's an order." He turns and starts walking.

My lashes lower and I want to push back, but Blake is gone now, and I need out of here now, tonight. And it appears that Lucifer is my only path to a quick face-off with Nick Waters, the Devils' founder—the devil incarnate himself.

I turn and start walking toward the black SUV at the curb, Adam, and Lucifer at my side. Adam heads to the passenger seat up front, the bastard. I climb in the rear, and Lucifer is already there on the other side.

Savage is behind the wheel. "You aren't leaving me out, motherfucker. I'm going with."

"You're married, Savage," I remind him. "You don't want in on this."

"Someone has to keep you from ending up dead," he argues. "And I'm born and raised in Texas. I know Texas. Lucifer and Adam don't." I open my mouth to argue and he shoots me the finger. "That's for whatever you were about to say. We're brothers now, even if you do tell stupid jokes." He starts to turn and pauses. "I packed you a bag. Thanks for putting me on your approved list with your building security." He settles back into his seat and starts driving.

I curse under my breath and buckle in for what I suspect is the beginning of what is going to be a helluva ride.

An hour later, we're in the air, and the ride is bumpy, the memories of two years undercover as a Devil, bumpier. But I've decided Lucifer's a godsend, at least behind the controls of a private jet. Savage is a pain my ass trying to find out where my head is, and Adam, well—Adam is Adam. He knows when to shut his mouth and just ride the bumps in silence.

We land at a private airport outside Austin and Blake has a downtown house rented for us, not far from where Priscilla lives. By Friday night, I'm damn glad we got out of New York when we did. The airports are shut, and yet, Team Walker is already at work here in Texas. Lucifer and Savage have headed out to hunt down the Devils' right-hand man, Jose Deleon, who is undoubtedly behind the murder of two witnesses. Meanwhile, Adam and I are going to watch Priscilla and decide if I'm going to testify.

My first glimpse of Priscilla is that morning, when she takes an early morning jog, her long, fit legs, and easy pace, establishing this as a normal routine. I jog with her but at a distance. She ends at a quirky little coffee shop by her house called Try Hard Coffee Roastery—Austin is full of quirky little places. I sit down at an outdoor table and wired to Adam, who's presently searching her house, I hit my mic. "She's wrapping up. How are you looking?"

"I was slow getting in. Buy me time."

"Copy that," I say, and since Priscilla doesn't know what I look like, I have nothing to hold me back.

I stand up and walk into the coffee shop, stepping behind her in the line only two deep, a good move since she's on the phone. "Yes, sir," she says. "I know, sir. I'm aware this is an election year. I'm aware that you're the first elected DA in Texas ever, but with all due respect, I'm not motivated by your re-election. I'm motivated by his heinous crimes."

Obviously, she's talking to the DA, Ed Melbourn, who I know from personal experience to be an arrogant asshole. A muffled, raised male voice lifts and reaches my ears. She holds the phone from her ear and when the shouting stops, replaces it and says, "I'll get him."

Apparently, Melbourn hangs up.

Priscilla makes a frustrated sound and shoves her phone back into a pocket on the side of her shorts. "Morning, Pri," the fifty-something redhead behind the counter calls out.

Priscilla or rather "Pri" hurries forward to greet her. "Morning, LouAnne."

Her shorts are red. Her voice is sweet. Her ass is sweeter. That doesn't mean she's sweet. In fact, some of the most dangerous people I've ever known had nice asses and cold hearts. I've never really found the idea of being fucked dead appealing.

"Your usual?" LouAnne asks her.

"I need a treat," Pri replies. "White mocha, please, skim milk, but hit me with the whipped cream."

"You got it, honey. I'll charge your account."

Pri heads down the counter to wait on her drink.

I lay cash on the table. "Same as her. It sounded good."

"How cute," she says, whatever the fuck that means. "But it's a good choice. It's the best drink we have."

"Keep the change," I say. "I'm sure it'll be worth it."

I step away from the register and find Pri staring at the television, watching a cooking show, of all things when she doesn't strike me as the domestic type. I'm now at the pick-up counter when she speaks to the woman next to her, who is also watching the show. "These shows make me wish I could cook."

The woman casts her a sideways look. "That bad, huh?"

"I'm horrible," Pri says. "I gave up years ago."

The male coffee barista calls out, "White mocha."

WHEN HE'S DIRTY

Pri turns and reaches for the cup, I reach for it as well. I did, after all, order a white mocha.

Chapter Three

ADRIAN

My hand collides with Pri's hand and a second later, I have my first close-up with the woman holding my future in her reach. And holy fuck, when her pretty blue eyes framed by long, dark lashes meet mine, I feel an unexpected, sharp pang of charge between us that has no place in this encounter.

"Oh, sorry," she says, jerking her hand back and giving a nervous laugh. "I ordered a white mocha, I thought that was mine."

She's beautiful, polite even, and everything male in me roars to life. "Per the barista we very adorably ordered the same drink, but you were in front of me. I didn't realize you didn't have your drink yet." I offer her the drink. "What kind of a gentleman would I be if I didn't wait my turn?"

"White mocha!" the barista calls out.

She smiles, and it's charming as hell. "Now we both have our drinks."

My lips curve. "I guess we do."

I offer her my hand and my brother's name. "Rafael Ramos," I say, using my brother's stage name, the lie told by necessity, not choice. I'm trying to stay alive, and I may be the person who keeps her alive. Or not. That's still to be determined.

She accepts my hand and the charge between us is back and instant. She feels it too, her lashes lowering, as if she's trying to hide her response, her gaze slowly lifting. "Priscilla Miller," she says, and when I reluctantly, and I do mean reluctantly, release her hand, she adds, "but call me Pri. It's not much better than Priscilla, but then everything is better than Priscilla."

"Nice to meet you, Pri. You hate the name that much, huh?"

"Oh yes," she confirms. "My mother had a thing for Priscilla Presley, as in Elvis's ex." She holds up a hand. "Don't ask. I don't understand either."

"What do you do, Pri?"

"I'm an attorney. What about you?"

"Private security," I say because the truth is, I'm going to face her as the real me, sooner than later. I'd prefer to do so with as few lies between us as possible. "What kind of law do you practice?"

"Criminal. I'm an Assistant DA." Her brows dip with an obvious thought. "Rafael. There's a singer named Rafael. You look like him. You're not—"

"No," I say, cursing my brother, who makes me proud as hell, but his newly escalated popularity in the states is not in my favor right about now. "But," I add, "I get that a lot."

"Priscilla!"

At the shout of her name, Pri turns away and then rotates right back to me, literally grabbing my arm, which is a surprisingly intimate gesture, not that I'm complaining. In fact, color me intrigued. "My God," she whispers urgently, "it's my mother. I can't be alone with her. Please help. Pretend to be my date?"

I arch a brow. "Pretend to be your *date*?"

"Please?"

17

Oh, how I'd like her to say please again, and for many other reasons. "What do I get in return?"

"Priscilla, honey."

Pri's eyes plead with me and she says, "Name your price—*later*."

She turns and her mother wraps her in a hug. "God, I'm so worried about you." She pulls back to study Pri. "You look horrible."

"Thanks for pointing that out, Mom." She grimaces and she even does that pretty. "I just went running," she adds. "I have on no make-up."

Her mother's eyes find mine and there is no question Pri is her mother's daughter, her eyes just as blue, her skin just as porcelain. Mother Pri gives me a once over, taking in my sweats and T-shirt, lingering on the ink on my arms, a tight inspection before she says, "Oh. My. You do pretty well for no make-up, honey. Muscles. Tattoos. Tall, dark, and good looking. *Who is this?*"

Pri face palms and amused, I say, "Rafael, and I don't have on any make-up either."

She laughs. "You're funny. I'm Amanda, Pri's mother."

"Nice to meet you," I say, but she's already dismissed me to scowl at Pri. "I like him. Does he know he's in danger just being near you?"

Pri's cheeks flush, her hands going up. "Okay stop, Mom," she bites out, low but tight. "Please. Rafael doesn't need you to scare him off. I can do just fine myself." She motions to her face. "I look horrible, remember?"

"You look great," she says. "Always. I'm critical right now because I'm worried about you. I'm looking for signs of stress." She pauses for effect. "I'm sorry. Please come back to the firm. Drop this case."

"No," Pri says, and I can sense the strain between them, as if they were once close, but there's now a wall between them. "And you should be happy," she adds. "I've given you an excuse to go hide out in Paris for a couple of months. Why are you still here?"

"We're leaving tomorrow," her mother assures her. "Come with us."

"No, Mother," Pri bites out, prim but firm. "I have a case. An important case and right now, I'm with Rafael."

I sip my coffee and arch a brow.

"Right," Amanda says, glancing in my direction. "Please protect her."

The plea hits a nerve, about ten, actually, that all tie back to my failure to kill the King Devil. Now people who didn't have to die are dead. "I will," I promise and I mean it—if she's one of the good guys.

Amanda motions to Pri. "Can we talk?"

"So you can tell me why dad and I should talk and why I should drop this case and come back to the firm?"

"Yes, actually."

"No to all of those things," Pri says, "but I still love you. Text me your flight info and I'll see you off."

Amanda sighs. "You win. I'll leave. I'll just go get my coffee." She hugs Pri, "I love you, too, sweetie." She eyes me over Pri's shoulder and releases her daughter. "Nice to meet you, Rafael."

I give her a nod and she walks away. Pri steps in front of me, close, but not close enough as far as I'm concerned. "I'm so sorry. Can we step outside, beyond her prying eyes and ears?"

"Of course."

"Thank you."

She turns and starts walking toward the door with purpose, offering me another delicious view of her perfect ass in the process. My lips curve, and I follow her, a predator with his prey in his sights, and soon we're outside, the day heating up because in Texas it's always heating up—the undercurrent of heat between us, even hotter.

"Thank you," she says, the minute we're outside behind a wall offering us privacy from the indoor guests. She rotates to face me, her breasts thrust high, every one of her many lush curves tempting my mouth and hands, but my attraction to her does nothing to dismiss my distrust. "And I'm so sorry I did that to you," she adds. "You don't even know me, but I'm good to my word. What do I owe you?"

The list of requests I could make right now are long and detailed, the most PG: dinner. Every male part of me wants to ask her out, to get to know her on the most intimate of levels—a plan I could justify easily as a means to establishing her true intent, but I'd be full of shit. It's the wrong move, the move Adrian Mack of the Devils would make. I am not that man. I will never be him again.

Already, she's going to be pissed when she finds out who I am and that is coming sooner rather than later. Already, I've ensured she will hate me when the real me is identified. Asking her out, leading her on, would be a death wish for me, at least with her. And right now, for all I know, she's aiding Waters, the King Devil himself, who does want me dead.

"You owe me nothing," I say. "I was just teasing you on that. I don't believe in debts."

There's a hint of what I believe is surprise in her eyes. "Most people take where they can take."

"Agreed," I say. "Why is she so worried?"

"I'm prosecuting a very bad man."

"Why is he bad?" I ask.

"Let me count the ways."

"You're not afraid?"

She folds her arms in front of her, a protective stance. "Terrified."

I arch a brow. "And you're still moving forward?"

"Someone has to." She drops her arms, "And I mean, they really *have* to."

"Because he's bad," I say and it's not a question. He is bad.

"Very bad. And I care. I want to make a difference. It's not political or showboating for me. I need to do this and do it well."

I believe her. She's motivated. She cares. But I'm also attracted to her, really fucking attracted to her, and I've learned the hard way that when it comes to people when it gets personal, fact-checking is lifesaving.

Adam's voice sounds in my ear, "I'm out. All clear. And so far, so is she."

I don't reply to him. Instead, I study Pri, searching my gut for a bad reaction that doesn't follow. "I changed my mind," I say. "You do owe me."

Her lips part and her head tilts, anticipation in her expression. "All right. What do I owe you?"

"The next time I see you here, you let me buy you a cup of coffee."

Surprise, and then pleasure, seeps into her eyes, curving her lips. "Deal."

I know this is where she expects me to set that date, but I don't do that. I can't do that. Instead, I lean in closer, a little closer, not near as close as I'd like and I say, "You look sexy as hell without make-up." I wink and turn away, leaving her standing there.

Chapter Four

PRISCILLA

When was the last time I looked into a man's eyes and felt my stomach flutter?

The answer: too long to remember before today.

I leave the coffee shop, coffee in hand, and during the three-block walk to my house, I'm still reliving my encounter with Rafael, replaying every word spoken, every casual touch that didn't feel casual at all. Of course, my mother showed up, and Rafael was too sharp not to notice the tension. I'm definitely not the girl who takes a man home to the family, especially since my ex, whose still the son my father never had, would likely be there.

Arriving at my house, I disarm the alarm, enter, and shut the door, listening for any sound that might not belong, and when my nerves are eating away at me, I reset the alarm and then yank open the drawer to the table by the door, and remove my handgun. This is insane. If I'm going to keep doing this job, I need to move to a high-security apartment. I try to remind myself that not every case involves the King Devil, as Waters calls himself, but that's hard to digest. My life is the devil right now, and people keep dying. No. They keep getting killed. Witnesses are dying. I'm not a witness, but I do have a responsibility to ensure they're protected and that the people the Devils hurt find some justice.

I ease down the hallway and good Lord, I can't stop myself. I call out, "Hello? Anyone here?" As if a killer would just say, "Oh, hi there, Pri, I'm in here in the kitchen." Angry at my stupidity, I stiffen my spine and head down the hallway, my tennis shoes soft on the search of the house. When I'm certain it's clear, I set the gun on my teal kitchen island and pull up a stool in front of my MacBook to check my messages before I shower. I quickly scan my inbox, hoping to hear from Agent Pitt about former FBI Agent Adrian Mack. Mack was inside the Devils' operation, close to Waters. His testimony can take Waters down. He's the one man between Waters and freedom.

I press my hands to my face. This case is huge. I have a team of people working with me, and while the DA manages every step I take and runs the case from the golf course. The pressure is immense and now, the danger, extreme. At least if I'd been an FBI agent, I could go to work with my weapon on my person. I'm licensed to carry but in my role, a gun at my hip, could be called intimidation. It certainly works against easing the nerves of witnesses. Instead, it's hidden in my purse, which isn't close enough for comfort right now.

I sip my coffee, which is now cold, and toss it in the trash before I dial Agent Pitt. He doesn't answer. Of course, he doesn't answer. He's the only link I have to Adrian Mack, who's been in hiding for over two years. He's supposed to be locating Mack for me. Why would he actually take my call?

For reasons I cannot explain, especially right now, of all times, in the middle of a killer case, quite literally, my mind is back on Rafael. I quickly google "Rafael," looking for the singer, who seems to have no last name, and the first image I pull up has my lips parting. My God, I was right. He *really does* look like the man I just met, only not quite like him. The resemblance is uncanny though and just to be sure, I google Rafael's, as in the singer's, tattoos. I couldn't quite make out all of the ink on my Rafael, but I know that it was black and red.

My gaze rakes over the singer's naked upper torso, and his ink is brightly colored, which means he is not my Rafael. The singer Rafael does have really amazing ripped abs and I wonder if my Rafael has those abs. I'm fairly certain the answer is yes. I'm one hundred percent certain that I'd like to find out. My phone rings and I glance at the number to find Grace, a co-worker, fellow assistant DA, and friend, who wants me at a party tonight. I'd ignore the call, except she's a good friend, the kind I never had back at the firm and it's her birthday. "Hey," I say, answering the call.

"How's it going?"

"It's—going," I say. "Happy birthday. Again."

She laughs. "I still can't believe you called me at midnight."

"And woke you up," I say. "I didn't think you'd be asleep on a Friday night."

"Alas, I'm becoming boring. I can't believe Josh's party is tonight of all nights. You're going, right?"

Josh is not only a detective who works for the DA like we do, albeit outside any direct contact with me, he's the detective Grace has long had a crush on but avoided because of the conflict of interest. And since he's now taking a job with a private security company to do the same work for more money, that problem has disappeared. I wonder briefly if he's going to work for the same company Rafael works for, but that's silly and an impossible coincidence.

24

Shoving aside my thoughts of a hot man I barely know, I go to work explaining myself to Grace. "I want to," I say, aware that she's shy outside of the courtroom and wants me with her.

"But?" she adds. "Why is there always a but with you?"

"I'm just a little worried about this case overflowing into my personal life."

"This isn't your personal life," she says. "It's work. We'll still be contracting Josh's services and he's someone we can trust. And the bar's going to be packed with cops and it's only a few blocks from work, which means your house. In other words, I can come to your door and get you."

"All right, all right" I concede. "I'll go for you."

"And *you*," she corrects. "You need a safe place to relax a little. It's September first. You have some time. The trial doesn't start for a month. I still can't believe this trial is going to run so close to the holidays."

"Had two of my witnesses not been murdered, we'd be starting sooner," I remind her. "And thankfully the judge understands that if we wait until the new year, everyone who ever touched this case might be dead."

"Yep. I was right. You need a drink."

"Yes," I agree. "I believe I do."

We chat a minute more and disconnect, and when I'm done, I click off Rafael's photo. I don't have the luxury of thinking about some hot man I'll likely never see again. I pull up a photo of Waters, the King Devil. He's the only man who will have my attention until at least Thanksgiving.

Okay, there is one more man, I decide to focus on not much later. I spend the entire working day fixated on Jose Deleon, the Devils' second in command. He's missing and likely the person killing the witnesses, but we have no proof. He'd probably be the person to kill me if I became a target. That thought is enough to convince me I need that night out surrounded by cops. That sends me to my closet to fret over what you wear to a sort of work event.

I settle on a black skirt with a flare, a lacy, sleeveless black top, and black booties with a heel. I never feel like a girl without my heels.

I slide my favorite round black Gucci purse over my chest to hang at my hip. It was an extravagant gift my mother called a birthday gift, but I knew it was delivered out of guilt for her behavior after I left the firm. She was not only angry, she refused to talk to me for a full month which was more than a little painful. My mother still doesn't understand that gifts don't equal support, nor do they matter to me as they do to her, but I know she meant well. And I do adore the purse. It fits a petite firearm, a lipstick, and powder, as well as my wallet perfectly. A petite handgun is a girl's best friend, even above lipstick.

My cellphone rings and I slide it from the pocket of my skirt to find Grace calling. "My Uber is about two minutes from your house. I'm picking you up."

I smile to myself and say, "What if I told you I was naked in the bathtub?"

"I'd tell you to grab a towel and hurry up." She disconnects.

I laugh and head downstairs, happy for the ride. I might only be a few blocks from the Mexican cantina where the party is being held, but right now, walking a few blocks alone at night doesn't feel smart. Not that

I've been threatened, I remind myself. I'm simply paranoid, but then how can I not be right about now?

Once I'm at my door, I wait there until my phone rings again with Grace's number. I answer and she says, "I'm here. Do I need to come pick your towel color?"

I grin and exit my front door to find the car at the curb. Locking up and arming my security system, I hurry toward the vehicle and climb inside.

"You look stunning, my dear," Grace says.

Grace is thirty, blonde with green eyes, gorgeous, and presently wearing a little black dress that makes me feel better about my little black skirt.

"So do you," I say, eyeing her cleavage. "I'm quite sure you'll have Josh's full attention in that little number."

She waves me off. "I don't even care. I have cases stacked from the floor to the top of my head, and men are trouble. I'm not sure I have the energy right now to decide if I trust someone just to be disappointed. I know you understand."

Oh too well, I think, but work is my friend. I've really had no time to deal with the personal side of life these past two years. We pull up to the dimly lit cantina, with teal and pink as a theme. There are also beer cans hanging from the ceiling and music blasting, at present "Homesick" by Kane Brown is playing, and the words hit one of those personal notes I usually avoid. Only I don't feel homesick like I used to at all. My new life is where I belong, no matter how lonely at times, and how much my mother likes to believe otherwise.

Grace and I head to the bar area, which includes a dance floor, where we're greeted by co-workers and then end up at one of the tan wooden standup tables.

We've barely ordered margaritas when the music is cut and Josh is ordered to the center of the empty dance floor, while one of the senior homicide detectives I know well, Martin Morgan, holds a microphone. Martin is tall, blond, and muscular with a hard face and a scar on his mouth. Josh is a bit taller, with light brown hair, and strong, classically handsome features that engage plenty of female attention, including Grace's, who leans in close to me to whisper, "Do I have to trust him to lust after him?"

"First comes lust," I say, managing a serious tone, "later trust."

"Good point," she says, snatching up a chip. "Lust has to happen first."

I smile with the wishful look she casts in Josh's direction, and at the jokes and speeches a slew of people soon deliver, about and on behalf of Josh's retirement.

It's a fun time, but there's no question that by the time the formalities are over, I'll be feeling tipsy. The margarita is big, strong, and despite being barely touched, effective at delivering my buzz, which probably is aided by the fact that I actually don't remember what I ate today. I reach for another chip and Grace grabs my arm. "Josh is coming over here. I don't know if I should do this, Pri."

"Honey," I say, aware that she was hurt badly and not that long ago. I also know Josh has long shown interest and he seems like a good guy, better than most. "You'll know if it's right. Give yourself some freedom to find out."

"Right. You're right. I'm a grown-ass woman. I can figure things out." She rotates away from me to greet Josh.

Right about then, Detective Newton, a thirty-something redhead, who I've had the pleasure of working with on several cases, stops by my table and introduces his wife before they head to the dance floor. A few more people I know chat with me about work before Grace appears by my side again, and since she's out of breath, I decide she's been making out or dancing. Her lipstick is perfect, so dancing wins.

"Josh wants to get a table in the restaurant, the two of us. Are you—"

"I'm fine. Go. Have fun. Tell me all about it later."

"You're sure?" she asks anxiously.

"Positive."

She hugs me and whispers, "Take an Uber home. I don't want you walking alone."

And then she's gone. I have no idea why I feel a twist in my belly, but I recognize it as familiar—it's loneliness. I'm alone. And if I'm honest, it's become a bit empty. But how do I do this job and ever not be alone? It's not exactly proving to be safe. And for a lot of reasons, so many reasons, I need to do this job.

I sip my drink and prepare to leave when a Rafael song comes on. I'm instantly jolted back into my morning coffee encounter with another Rafael. And just like that, as if I've willed him into existence, he's standing next to me—tall, dark and gorgeous, in black jeans and a black T-shirt.

"Hi," he says softly.

"Hi," I reply.

"This seems like our song, don't you think?" He offers me his hand. "Dance with me?"

I'm charmed by his reference to me saying that he looks like Rafael. It's also a sexy song, too, and I oddly, considering how many men I deal with daily, feel a bit shy with this man but I still manage to say, "I think it might just be."

Yet I find myself hesitating to take his hand, and I don't know why. It's as if some part of me knows that touching him is a major decision, a life-changing decision when it's just a dance in a Mexican cantina. It's just a dance and still, I am blinking up at him, searching his face for answers, and what I find in his rich brown eyes is interest, intelligence, a connection I feel to my toes. And I know why I hesitate. I know why my hand lingers above his. This—him—we're bad timing. And right now, I'm toxic.

WHEN HE'S DIRTY

Chapter Five

PRISCILLA

I pull my hand back from Rafael's. "You don't want to dance with me."

He studies me, his head tilting slightly, his intelligent brown eyes searching mine. "You mean you don't want to dance with me." It's not a question, but rather his assessment.

"No," I say quickly. "Yes. I mean—thankfully, I'm a little less confusing in a courtroom than I am right now. Let me try again: it's not about what I want."

He steps closer, and he smells woodsy and masculine with a hint of spice, his scent teasing my nostrils and stirring my senses. It's been so long since a man stirred anything in me. "It's very much about what you want," he says, and even his voice—all low, rough baritone—does funny things to my belly. "I'm all about you right now," he adds.

My hand lifts and almost lands on his chest. I catch myself and when I would pull it back, he captures it, and his touch sizzles up my arm and across my chest. "I don't bite."

"And what if I do?"

His lips hint at a smile. "I'm fairly certain you do, but I'm also certain I'd enjoy it."

"You wouldn't. Not in the way I'm meaning it."

"Then why don't we use my definition, not yours?" His gaze lowers to my mouth, lingering there before it lifts. "If you need me to explain—"

"No," I say, feeling my cheeks heat. "I don't. How are you even here?"

"I assume we're new neighbors. I moved into the neighborhood this weekend. At least for a while, until I finish a work project."

"A security project?"

"Surveillance for now, but yes, and don't ask who."

I'm curious. I want to ask more. I settle on, "Okay. How long will you be here?"

"Long enough for me to buy you that coffee." He gives my hand a tug, and suddenly my leg is pressed to his. "Dance with me," he says.

My throat is cotton. My body is fire. "Our song ended."

"We'll find another," he promises.

"I liked that one."

"Why?"

"It meant something."

He pulls back, searching my face, and then, "What did it mean?"

I pull my hand from his and reach for my drink, and meet his eyes, sipping from the straw before I say, "I haven't decided yet."

His lips quirk, and he has very nice lips. "In other words," he says. "it's me you haven't decided on." He reaches for my straw and sips, his lips now where my lips just were, the very act suggestive—provocative. *He's* provocative and I seem to like it. He rests an elbow on the table, his forearm flat on the wood, the ink of his right arm abstract, gray and black tree limbs with red blossoms, I think. I want to know what is on his shoulder. I want to ask what the ink means.

Suddenly, I realize I'm staring, and my gaze jerks to his. "Does the ink bother you?" he asks.

"The opposite," I say, and it's true. The men in my life are all suits and ties kind of guys, who wouldn't dare a full sleeve of ink. And the world I'm in is ever-so-suffocating right now. "I like it," I dare.

He leans in a little closer. "Do I make you uncomfortable, Pri?"

"No," I say. "The fact that my co-workers are here makes me uncomfortable. And I make me uncomfortable right now. And I should make you uncomfortable. I didn't send my mother to Europe for no reason. That case I mentioned is high-profile and dangerous."

"And you think I'm dangerous?"

"No," I say. "I think *I'm* dangerous."

"Because of the case?"

"Yes. I expose you to that case just by having this conversation. I can't do this, whatever this is, right now."

"I understand," he says simply.

"You do?"

"I do, though I am curious about why you're doing something that obviously terrifies you. Is it simply your job? Is it because you have to do it?"

"It's like standing at the bottom of a mountain and deciding to climb it. Halfway up, you look down and you know you're going to fall, but you can't turn back."

"But you want to turn back?"

"No," I say without hesitation. "You want what you always wanted, to get to the top. Now, you just have to get to the top before you die."

His eyes go wide. "Die?"

"Sorry," I sip my drink. "I'm being dramatic."

He studies me, his eyes seeing too much, and I have this sense he might see more than anyone before him, perhaps more than I see myself. I want to look away. I don't want to look away. I'm conflicted, but when he reaches for me, I don't even think about pulling away. His finger brushes my cheek, a feather-light touch, and somehow I feel that touch all over my body. "I don't think you are," he says softly.

"Which is why I should leave. That and this is a work gathering. I can't do this. I'll see you at the coffee shop." I rotate to the other side of the table and hurry toward the bathroom, which I know is down a hallway by the bar.

Once I'm inside the one-stall bathroom, I press my hands to the counter and stare into the mirror. *What am I doing?* I don't know Rafael. I don't know if I can trust him. He could be a reporter who could tell the world I'm rattled by the case. I'm stupid. So very stupid. He's just—something, I don't know what—different, I decide. Different from anyone I know, or have known. And really hot. He's so incredibly hot and I've been alone for a long time. Since—I stop myself. I'm not going down that rabbit hole.

I use the bathroom, wash up, and decide that I'll walk home. I need to stop letting Waters be the devil that scared me into incompetence. It's three blocks and I have a gun that I know how to use. I exit the bathroom and halt to find Rafael standing in the doorway, his hands on either side of the doorframe. "What are you doing?"

"This," he says, and suddenly, his hands are on my waist, and he's walked me back into the bathroom.

Before I know what's happening, he's kicked the door shut, and his fingers are diving into my hair. "Kissing you, because I can't fucking help myself. And because you might not ever let me do it again. That is unless you object?"

That's the part that really gets me. The "unless I object," the way he manages to be all alpha and demanding and still ask. Well, and the part where he can't fucking help himself.

I press to my toes and the minute my mouth meets his, his crashes over mine, his tongue delivering a wicked lick that I feel in every part of me. He tastes of temptation with a hint of tequila, demand, and desire. His hands slide up my back, fingers splayed between my shoulder blades, his hard body pressed to mine, seducing me in every possible way.

I moan with the feel of him and his lips part from mine, lingering there a moment before he says, "Obviously, someone needs to protect you from me," he says. "Like me." And then to my shock, he releases me and leaves. The bathroom door is open and closed before I know what's happened. And once again, I have no idea if or when I will ever see him again.

⸺⸺⸺ ∞ ⸺⸺⸺

ADRIAN

Priscilla Miller tastes like heaven, which means she could easily drag me to hell. I can't forget that.

I'm at the side of the restaurant when Pri exits and I expect her to leave the way she arrived, by way of an Uber. She does not. She starts walking. Holy Mother of Jesus, what is she thinking? She knows she's in the hot seat. She knows she's a potential target for Waters. I curse under my breath, discreetly following her, when

I want to grab her, throw her over my shoulder and take her home to punish her, preferably without clothing.

Thank fuck the walk is short, and Adam's watching her house. I hang back across the street where I fade into the center of the bushes. I watch as Pri keys in the code to her lock and enters her house. Adam appears in the bushes next to me. "Who the hell is watching her house?"

"Lucifer," he says. "He's back. Savage is not. He's still looking for Deleon, but so far Blake is coming up dry and so is Savage. It's starting to seem like he's dead, too."

My jaw clenches. "He's not," I say. "I know him well. He's smart, he's a killer, and he's loyal to his king. He's here. He's just waiting for the right moment to take out his next victim."

"Is the Assistant DA helping to create his hit list or is she on it?"

"I don't know yet," I say, glancing over at him, "but she claims she's dangerous."

"And yet she walked home."

"She said she's dangerous, not that she's in danger."

He arches a brow. "Almost as if she's on Waters' payroll and knows she's safe?"

"Maybe," I say. "Maybe not."

He studies me a moment and says, "Just how close to her did you get?"

In other words, I think, he already knows. "You were watching."

"Too close, if you didn't tell her who you are."

"Not fucking close enough," I correct. "I still don't know which side she's on."

"Then what's the plan?"

"We watch her," I say.

"And you get *too* close again? Because we both know you're getting too close to her, man."

I don't deny the obvious. What's the point? "I haven't decided yet," I say.

His jaw clenches but he says nothing. He simply faces forward because he doesn't have to say anything else. We both know he's right. I got too close to Pri tonight. I'll pay a price with her later, but it seems there's still a little devil left in me, perhaps too much. Because as I confessed to Pri, I just couldn't fucking help myself.

WHEN HE'S DIRTY

Chapter Six

PRI

I wear my lucky suit Monday morning, the one with the navy flared skirt, a teal silk tank, and a jacket that hits right at the waist. Good things happen when I wear this suit. As silly as that might sound, it's true, and I'll take all the luck I can get. I'm at my desk by seven AM. By nine, I'm in a conference room with the team that's working on this case, staring at a whiteboard that lists our witnesses, and it doesn't look good. These are supporting witnesses who frame a bigger story, one with key, crucial witnesses, of which two are now dead.

Agent Pitt walks into the conference room, dressed in a suit, always Mr. Professional, at least in appearance. Behavior is a whole new story. He walks toward the conference table, clearly intending to take a seat and pretend he hasn't been ignoring my calls.

"Can I see you in my office?" I ask, right when he would sit down.

He freezes, a grimace on his handsome face before he glances my way. "Of course." He turns and exits the room, with me on his heels, but not for long. I take the lead, quickly walking down the hallway to enter my office. By the time I'm behind my desk, he's shut the door and he steps just behind the visitor's chairs.

"I really, really don't appreciate you ignoring my calls," I say.

"I don't report to you, Miller. I was on duty, working a case."

"Do you intend to actually prosecute someone in that case, unlike this one?"

He's back to grimacing. "Is this really how you want to start the day?"

I press my hands to my desk. "Witnesses are dead, which only adds to Waters' body count. People are *dead*. I'm doing this to give them the justice they deserve. I need Adrian Mack."

"You think I don't know people are dead, Pri?" he snaps. "I worked with Adrian for two years, trying to take Waters down. I saw what Waters is capable of. And I'm brutally aware of the body count Waters created, directly and indirectly, which tallies to dozens. As for Adrian, he wanted your file."

"My file? What does that even mean?"

"As you pointed out, witnesses are dead. He's a target. For all he knows, you're dirty or incompetent or both. He doesn't trust easily. Why do you think he's hiding out on his own?"

"Since the US Marshall's, aided by the FBI, can't seem to keep my witnesses alive, I'd say because he's smart."

"I'm going to pretend you didn't say that."

I run a hand under my hair, across my neck. "I'm sorry. I know you risk your life all the time. I know you're trying."

His hands settle under his jacket on his hips. "Adrian won't let us down, but he's going to check you out thoroughly before he comes forward."

"Why doesn't he just meet with me and judge me in person?"

"Give him time."

"I have no time," I argue.

"He might not even show up until right before the trial and you have to trust him to know what's right."

"Trust him? I'm not trusting anyone I've never even met."

"He knows Waters like no one else. He'll do what the has to do to protect himself and the prosecution. He's going to stay alive and we need him to stay alive."

"The DA wants to know I have a solid case."

"You do," he argues. "Even without Adrian, you do. No jury is letting that man go. We have solid evidence. We have other witnesses." He leans forward on the desk. "We're all tense. We're all targets. Fuck, I'm looking over my shoulder, too. I'm sure you are as well."

"I doubt I'm a target," I say. "I know only what is in the file."

"What better way to end a trial than to kill the lead attorney?"

"I'm not the only attorney on the case," I argue.

"Who else would want to take lead if you were dead?" He doesn't give me time to reply. "I can get you protection."

"As in someone following me around?"

"Yes."

The sickness of all I have discovered over Waters colors my reply. "No, and I'm not trying to be stupid. Waters has a habit of turning good cops bad. I'll trust myself over anyone else right now."

"You sure?" he asks, and the very fact that he doesn't deny my statement, validates my reply.

"Do you know something I should know?"

He pushes off the desk. "You know what I know. That's why I'm a witness."

"How did you leave it with Adrian?"

"I told him to hurry the fuck up and make a decision." He heads for the door and glances back at me. "If you change your mind on security—"

"I won't."

He nods and exits the office, leaving me with the realization that my top witness is investigating me. Unfortunately, he might not like what he finds.

"Miller."

I jolt and I look up to find Ed Melbourn, the DA standing in my doorway, a moment before he steps inside my office and shuts the door. He's fifty-something, fit, a big man, with thick salt-and-pepper hair, broad shoulders, and a broader presence.

"Where are we on the Waters case?"

"Exactly where anyone would be after two key witnesses were murdered," I answer, always direct and honest, which has served me well with Ed. I think. It's hard to know where you stand with Ed. "The team is rattled, but we're pushing forward, reframing our case. We can still win this."

"What about that FBI agent that was undercover with Waters?"

"He's not keen on coming forward, at least not now. Pitt seems to think he might be a last-minute addition."

"Last minute is not a good plan. What's his problem?"

"Two dead witnesses. He doesn't want to be dead right along with them. He doesn't trust law enforcement to protect him, and frankly, sir, I understand."

"What I understand is that we need Waters to go down."

"We still have a solid case," I argue.

"Until another witness ends up dead? Or has sudden memory loss? For all we know, they'll get on the stand and have that memory loss there. Your daddy's a beast. He does whatever it takes to win. Be your daddy, Miller." He opens the door and intends to exit.

"If I wanted to be my father, I'd still be working for him." It's out before I can stop it and I'm not sure I would have even tried.

He half turns and eyes me. "And yet, you got this case because of your track record with your daddy. If you lose it, some might think you can't make it without him. I will."

He turns and exits.

I rotate away from the desk, facing the wall, and give myself about two seconds of self-doubt before my spine stiffens and I rotate again and head for the door, intent on pursuing Ed. That's when Cindy, the newest ADA, straight out of school, and working under me, steps inside the office. She's petite, feisty, and a pretty blonde who has proven to be a real asset. "Zara Moore, Waters' ex-girlfriend, says she's no longer willing to testify. She remembers nothing."

I can almost feel a fist punch me right in the chest. "Where is she now?"

"She left protective custody. That's all I know. What now?"

"We find another witness," I say, but I already know we're out of options. Except one: Adrian Mack.

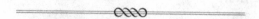

About six-thirty, Cindy and I head to the coffee shop by my house, the scent of fresh baked cookies stirring old memories of a nanny who baked often, while my mother did not. But to my mother's credit, she did love to eat the tasty treats over shared story time while my father was always at work.

For now, I pass on my cookie craving, and Cindy and I order drinks, before spending another hour working. "Three key witnesses feels like enough," she says, as we're wrapping up.

"It should be," I say, "but my gut says Zara won't be the last witness to get cold feet."

"Or die?" she asks. "Talk about being intimidated in a big way. This case has gotten outright creepy. Do you ever get worried we're on the hitlist, too?"

I sip what's left of my coffee, and do so with the intent of hiding my reaction. Pitt said the same thing. It's not a pretty idea, not at all. In fact, it's an ugly idea.

"You're fine," I assure her, setting my cup down. "And this is the best way to start. Everything you face after this case will feel a little less intimidating."

"Do you still get intimidated? I mean, you worked on some really big cases in the private arena."

"Every time I take a case, I affect someone's life. Every time, I'm intimidated by the great, but welcomed burden and responsibility to do right by people who have only me to count on."

"Yes," she says. "I can see that. If I didn't want to do right by people, I wouldn't be working for pennies. I could have taken a job with a firm for more money. But I,"—her lips purse together—"it feels a bit political here, doesn't it?"

"Everything's a little political," I say. "And I don't worry about the DA pressuring me for a win if the victim's guilty. If he wasn't guilty, that would be another story. Or if this was another case and the victim was innocent and he was forcing me to convict."

"What would you do if he forced you to convict an innocent man?"

"Refuse. You decide who you are, Cindy, and your choices reflect who you are."

"But if it's my job—"

"This isn't just a job. It's a moral obligation and if you can't be on the right side of your morals, well, I guess that's really between you and your maker."

She studies me a moment and then says, "You're a good influence."

"I haven't always been. Go home. We have some busy days ahead of us."

"What about you?"

There is a punch in my gut at the idea of walking into my house alone. "I'm going to grab another coffee and take some notes before I leave."

"I can wait."

"I'm good. Go home."

She grabs her things and right before she stands, she says, "I'm glad our paths crossed." She doesn't wait for a reply. She heads for the door.

I'm a good influence. I doubt Adrian Mack is going to think that when he digs into my history. Which means I can't count on him to show up. All the more reason to stay awhile and find the holes I need to plug in this case. Leaving my things behind—I'm the only one in here right now—I walk to the counter, pay for another coffee and splurge on a giant iced sugar cookie. I might not have a man in my bed, which is perpetually empty, despite that kiss in the bathroom, but my belly will be full this night. And I can run off the cookie. The wrong man tends to be a bit harder to recover from, as I've proven quite decisively.

With my cookie in hand, I turn away from the register and find myself running smack into a hard body. "Oh God. I'm sorry." My hands land on a hard wall of muscle and I glance up to find Rafael staring down at me, amusement in his brown eyes.

"Don't be," he says. "I'm not."

Chapter Seven

PRI

My beautiful new neighbor is back with his goatee, dark hair, and chiseled features looking better than ever, right here in my favorite coffee shop, standing so close. The mix of masculine spice and freshly baked sugar cookies is ridiculously, unexpectedly erotic. So much so that I have to remind myself that I've made an enemy of the King Devil, and who better to send to watch me, set me up, or even kill me than a beautiful monster? He's also still touching me and I yank my hands back. "I should get my coffee."

I start to turn and he catches my elbow, and Lord help me, heat rushes up my arm and across my chest. As if that's not enough, my nipples pucker beneath the lace of my bra. "What just happened?" he asks. "Why are you running from me?"

Damn him for being so perceptive, or maybe damn me for being so obvious. "Nothing. I just wanted to let you order." He glances at the manager. "Whatever she had," he says, tossing a twenty on the counter. "Keep the change."

All the while, he's *still* touching me and I don't know why I'm not pulling away. His attention returns to me, though somehow I feel as if it was always on me, even when he was looking away, his body shifting just enough to shelter me from the manager's eyes, as he softly asks, "Is this about the kiss?"

"No. Yes. I mean no." My lashes lower and then lift, "God, what is it about you that makes me forget how to make a point?" I don't wait for his reply. "It's not the kiss. The kiss was—" I hesitate, not sure how to finish that sentence, considering where I'm at in my life right now.

He arches a brow. "It was?" he prods, not about to let me off the hook on this one, clearly.

I don't make him push hard and with good reason. I hate lies and games, so I speak honestly, "Good and bad. The bad is that now is not a good time for this." I twist away from him, grab my coffee and head to my seat. Once I'm settled behind my computer, I sip my coffee, which is a butterscotch latte. It's an acquired taste, and I'm aware that Rafael just ordered what I ordered. Somehow, I'm watching as he retrieves his order and I tell myself to look away, I do, but he's addictive, pure sex. I thought I favored men in suits, but not so much right about now. Now, I seem to favor denim, tattoos peeking from T-shirt sleeves, and boots. His jeans and T-shirt are both dark blue and snug enough that I can appreciate his broad shoulders and perfect ass.

He begins to turn and I quickly eye my computer screen, sipping my coffee. About twenty seconds later, he slides into the seat across from me, setting his cookie and cup on the table. When I look up, I melt in a pool of his warm chocolate brown eyes as he says, "Here's a good reason to get to know me."

I smile. "Okay. What's the good reason?"

"I tell bad jokes and I laugh at them so you don't have to."

But I do indeed laugh. "Okay," I say. "I'll bite. Tell me a bad joke."

"You didn't think that was a joke?"

"You can do better," I challenge, surprised at how easily I've relaxed into the moment with a man I've only just met.

"Okay," he says. "You asked for it." He pretends to roll up his non-existent sleeves, and I notice the skull in the midst of a sleeve of tattoos on his left arm. He sips his coffee. "Butterscotch," he says. "I like it. I'm inspired to tell a really stupid joke." I smile and he adds, "We're in Texas A&M joke territory so that's where I'm headed. Did you hear about the Aggie who won a gold medal at the Olympics? He was so proud of it he got it bronzed."

I laugh. "That was indeed cheesy."

"I specialize in cheesy. And it *did* make you laugh."

"Yes. Thank you. I needed that, actually."

He leans in closer, sobering as he does. "About our timing."

Our timing, I repeat in my mind. There is something about the way he represents us as one that does funny things to my belly. "What about it?" I ask.

"I've learned that now is always better than later. There might not be a later."

He hits ten nerves all at once. "Exactly," I whisper rather fiercely. "I want you to have a later. And me, too."

His eyes narrow, sharpen. "What does that mean? Talk to me, Pri."

"I don't even know you," I remind him. "And you don't know me."

"I want to know you. Do you want to know me?"

He wants to know me. I want to know him. Instead, I say, "I told you. Now is not a good time."

"Now is exactly the right time. *Do you want to know me?*"

"I don't know if I can trust you."

He studies me a long moment, his eyes never leaving my face. "I work for Walker Security. Check us out." He picks up a pen and scribbles information on the napkin. "That's us," he says, sliding the napkin in front of me. "I gave you our company name and Blake Walker's number. He's one of the founding brothers and my direct boss. He'll be easy to check out. He's widely respected, even as high up as the White House."

"White House?" I ask, ever so curious now. "What exactly does Walker do?"

"We handle protection, recovery, even airport security, and supplement law enforcement investigations at all levels. Check the references."

"Even if I do, and they're all wonderful, that doesn't mean you, or people around you, can't be bought."

He tilts his head, and quite astutely says, "You think someone close to you is dirty?"

"The defendant loves to turn good people into bad people, including law enforcement. Witnesses in protective custody have died. Others are running scared. What do you think?"

"And you think you're a target?"

"An FBI agent told me to watch my back because I could be a target today. So yes, I do."

"I'm ex-FBI. That doesn't mean you're a target. It could be a power trip. It could be pure caution. If there was a real threat, you'd be under protective custody. What does the DA say?"

"He says to win the battle. We have to win. And I don't disagree. It's the King Devil of the Devils biker club. He's bad, really bad. Evil, even."

He studies me a moment, no perceivable reaction as I might expect. In fact, all he says is, "Are you going to make him pay?"

"Yes," I say, firming my words, wanting to convince us both. "I am."

Approval lights his eyes, and his mouth, which has been on my mouth, curves. "Then let's eat a cookie and celebrate."

"The cookie is for the pre-trial stress. The jury giving him life and a hundred years is a champagne celebration."

"Well then, it's a date. Champagne to celebrate."

A date, I think. That is somehow so much more than a kiss in the bathroom. "I doubt you'll be around when this is over," I say, sipping my coffee. "If we're lucky, we'll be done by Thanksgiving, but I doubt it."

"I'll be here," he promises, taking a bite of his cookie and I do the same, before he says, "Hmm. Damn good cookie. I forgot how good everything tastes in Texas." His lips quirk and it's clear that he's not talking about the cookie.

Heat spikes between us and with good reason. He wants me to think about his fingers in my hair and his mouth on my mouth, and it works. I do. God, how I do. I shift in my seat and ask, "Where do you live now?"

"Walker's based out of New York City, but I'm hardly ever home. I'm always away on a job. Last year, I spent a few months in Europe, traveling with an heir to the Stradivari empire."

"Really? Wow. The Stradivari family? As in the famous violin makers?"

"Yes. That was her."

"That's amazing. Maybe one day you can actually tell me about it."

"One day," he says. "You mean when you're past seeing me as the bad guy, I will."

"I don't see you as the bad guy."

"Then let me walk you home," he counters.

"I still don't know you."

"Let me rephrase: I'm not letting you walk home alone."

"I can take an Uber." I laugh bitterly. "But I guess the Uber driver could be my assassin, too. And at least I know you smell good."

He smiles. "I smell good."

"Well, you did the other night. I'm pretty sure you smell the same way I do tonight—essence of coffee beans."

"Well, here's my pitch: the good news is that, aside from my alluring coffee bean smell, I have skills. I'll get you home safely."

"Unless you're here to kill me."

"Without another taste?" he says. "*Never.*"

He's flirting and I'm falling under his spell, which is why I say, "I have a gun. I know how to use it."

His lips quirk. "Good. That's good. I'll be sure to ask before I kiss you again."

"You asked the first time."

His voice lowers, "And you said yes. Say yes now to me walking you home."

There is something about this man, something that draws me to him and pulls me under in all the ways a woman wants to be pulled under. The timing might be horrible, but somehow, it's just right. It's perfect. It's what I need. He is that little escape I need.

"Yes," I say. "Please walk me home."

Chapter Eight

PRI

Now that I've decided to trust Rafael and let him walk me home, I'm relieved for the company, proof that Agent Pitt's warning is wearing on me. I shut my MacBook and put my work into my briefcase before pulling out my flats from my bag, and holding them up for Rafael to see. "These are so you don't have to pick me up from the ground." I replace my heels with my comfy walking slippers and stand up. Rafael does the same, and now we're both at the end of the table, so close we're almost touching, every part of me hyperaware of his closeness.

"You're very tall," I say, glancing up at him, hiding how affected I am by him with words.

"You're very short," he counters.

"Not when I have on my heels."

His lips quirk. "I did have to lean down a little less last night than I would tonight to kiss you."

As if I'm a schoolgirl, something about this moment heats my cheeks.

"But I promise not to kiss you tonight," he says. "I won't kiss you again until you trust me." He picks up my bag. "And as proof, I'll carry this. Your hands will be free, but mine won't be. You're safe."

Safe he says, I think. I'm fairly certain there is nothing safe about this man, at least on a wholly personal level.

"Thank you," I say, a little disappointed about the kiss, but also charmed by his reasoning.

We head outside, and with August barely behind us, the night is still warm and muggy, in the high seventies. "You said you moved here in the area?" I ask as we fall into step together.

"I am," he says. "I'm in a house on Plum Street."

"Oh well, that's super close to my place, a few blocks at most."

"How long have you been in the neighborhood?" he asks.

"Since I graduated college and started law school. I wish I could say I bought it on my own, but I didn't. My house was a gift from my parents."

He casts me a sideways look. "That's very generous of them."

"Not really," I say. "I mean *it was*. Don't get me wrong, I don't mean to seem like a spoiled brat, but my father does things to get things."

"And what did he get?"

"Me working for his law firm."

"Aren't you with the DA?"

"I am, but I only joined the DA two years ago. I made a lot of money working with my father, but I wasn't happy."

"And you're happy now?" he asks, casting me a curious look.

"I don't know if I'd call it happy, but I have a purpose. I fight for people who need me to fight for them. What about you? Why Walker and not the FBI now?"

"A bit of the same," he says, "with a bit of reversal. I make good money with Walker and do right by people every time."

"And you didn't do right by people every time at the FBI?"

"No," he says, cutting his stare before he glances back at me, and uses Walker to shift the topic rather abruptly back to me. "You mentioned everyone could turn dirty. Walker makes sure we have *every* reason to stay loyal. And it's not just the money. We're a family."

The word "family" hits me hard.

That's what I thought I'd feel at my father's firm. I didn't. I motion to my house. "That's me. My front door's on the side of the house. Weird, I know."

We head down a sidewalk, and once we're at the door, I key in the security code and open the door before facing him. "Thank you for walking me home. I think that warning I got today to be careful got to me more than I'd like it to have."

"You want me to check out the inside?" he offers, and before I can answer he adds, "Don't worry. I'm a man of my word. I've already promised that I'm not going to kiss you tonight. Obviously, that means we aren't getting naked. None of *that* right now."

In other words, I think, we might later, and as direct as this comment is, I appreciate the honest and bold way about him, something genuine I've experienced so little in my life. "All right then," I say. "Yes, please. You checking things saves me running around with a gun in my hand on my own."

There's a shift in the air, a darkening to his mood. "That's what you're doing every time you enter your house?"

"He's the King Devil, Rafael. And I almost believe he's the *real* devil."

He studies me for a few intense beats, in which I think he might say something, but he seems to think better of it. Instead, he glances inside the house, sets my bag on the floor in the foyer, and then catches my hand, an electric charge spiking up my arm. "Come inside the door." He backs up and takes me with him, shutting the door behind him. "I'll be right back," he promises, and then he's gone.

I lean on the wall and watch him disappear into the house, his strides long, confident, and I hold my breath, counting down until he reappears. "All clear," he says, and as he closes the space between me and him, there's a predatory grace about him. Right now, as he steps in front of me, I feel like his prey. And oddly, it doesn't scare me.

He leans a hand on the wall beside me, his gaze sliding over my mouth and I know he's thinking of kissing me, but his eyes lift and he says, "I wrote my number next to Blake's. If anything feels off, anything at all, call me."

"Thank you," I say.

"You say thank you a lot."

"Is that bad?"

"No," he says. "Just an observation. You're beautiful, smart, brave, and polite. All observations."

And all amazing compliments, I think. "Do you want my observations about you?" I ask.

"No," he surprises me by saying. "I don't." There's a sudden, hard edge to his voice, as he pushes off the wall. "And because I'm a man of my word," he adds, "I'm going to leave before I forget why I wasn't going to kiss you. Good night, Pri."

He opens the door and exits, leaving me alone and while I'm used to being alone, for the first time in a very long time, I wish I wasn't.

∞

ADRIAN

The minute I'm outside the range of Pri's security cameras, I dial Blake. "Adrian," he answers. "Talk to me. How's Texas?"

"Priscilla Miller, the ADA on Waters' case should be calling you and asking about Rafael, which would be me."

"Holy fuck," he snaps. "What the hell are you thinking? Who does she think Rafael is?"

"I told her I'm with Walker Security, but as far as she's concerned, we're new, friendly neighbors."

"How friendly?"

"I'm just trying to keep us both alive."

"How fucking friendly?" he demands and then says, "Never mind. I can read that answer loud and fucking clear. What happens when she finds out who you really are? You do see the problem here, right?"

I scrub my jaw. "Yeah, I get that, Blake, and I feel like shit about misleading her, but she's scared."

"You think you playing games with her makes that better?"

"I'm not playing a fucking game. I'm trying to keep us all alive, her included. Either she's afraid because witnesses are dying or—"

"Waters promised to kill people she loves if she doesn't do his bidding," he supplies.

"Exactly. I have to know which to know how to help her."

"I'll do some digging," Blake says. "And if she calls me? Where do you want this to go?"

"She seems to think Waters got to some insiders. I led her to Walker as an escape, a way to protect her witnesses. If she calls, I'll know she's not compromised."

"The DA has to approve the finances. I'm not sure that's a good indicator."

"I know Ed. He's a self-serving, power-hungry bastard. It's an election year and this is a giant case. He'll approve it. And if I read her right, she'll call you and give you a chance to help her sell it."

"And when are you coming clean with her?"

"After we get Walker approved and on the case officially. Waters has to go down. We're the way everyone who can make that happen stays alive."

"If that's how you want to play this, you can't meet with Ed. Who do you want on this?"

"Adam. He's a chameleon. He's our man."

"All right, but, Adrian—don't drag this out. This only gets dirtier the longer you deceive Priscilla." *Pri*, I silently correct, but it doesn't matter. Blake disconnects and I curse. He's right. I'm treading water here, about to drown in sugar cookies and Pri Miller. I let this get personal with Pri when it didn't have to be, but somehow it's fitting. Everything about taking down Waters is personal, including protecting Pri. She can hate me, but she won't get rid of me, not until this is over.

With my resolve firmly in place, I head to the rental house Blake lined up for us, and until now I've given very little thought of. In a short walk, the two-story slate gray house with a steepled roof probably runs a cool million. In Austin, that doesn't mean you get a lot of house, not in this zip code. In other words, Pri's parents gifted her an expensive property. She left their law firm but stayed in the house. I don't want that to matter, but if she were anyone else, I'd be thinking about her position on money. Once you have a taste, it's hard to walk away, even if you think you can, but I rule that out as a concern. I heard her with her mother. She could go back to the firm and make money again.

Money doesn't motivate her.

She can't be bribed, which means Waters would either kill her or threaten to kill someone close to her.

I walk through the side gate of the house and around back, entering directly into the kitchen, and step onto the gray varnished concrete floors that flow through the entire house. The living room to the left is empty and I spy a bag of Oreos on the top of the large marble island with my name on them.

Adam charges into the room before I get the chance, his voice low, but his agitation tics along his jawline. "What the hell are you doing, A?"

Grimacing, I grab the Oreos and snatch one. "Eating a cookie. I'm starving." I inhale my cookie, and I'm ready for another. I reach for the bag.

He snatches it from my hand and sets them out of my reach. "What are you *doing*?"

"I don't know if I should be pleased or irritated that Blake works this fucking fast."

"You know what," he says, sliding the cookies back in my direction, "eat up. You need something to shut you up, *Rafael*."

I ignore the cookies and open the fridge, grabbing two beers and handing him one. "I did what I had to do."

"You think she'll see it that way?"

"Not a chance in hell," I say, and not because of the name game I'm playing. Because I was a devil, and I lived like one. Because while there are laws to protect me, I pushed those limits, and I know it. I need immunity to even take the stand and she's going to have to give it to me. Which means Pri's going to have to know my sins to forgive them.

Chapter Nine

PRI

I take a cold shower after Rafael leaves, a cliché meant for men, of course, but I'm desperate to think about my work, not the hot man I wanted to kiss me, the man who didn't kiss me. Maybe he didn't want to kiss me or maybe he really wants my trust. Either way, by the time I'm in boxers and a tank, microwaving a Lean Cuisine, I've decided I want to trust him, but I can't let my guard down. I've read too many stories about Waters' devious ways.

I've just settled onto my bed with my gun next to me, my dinner, a glass of wine, and my work sprawled out around me when my mother calls. "Hi, Mom. When's your flight?"

"We're not going. Your father has a big case that just fell in his lap and I'm not leaving him here alone."

I set my food aside and sit up, legs back on the floor. "Mom, it's dangerous. This case is dangerous."

"We can't run every time you have a dangerous case. And I don't have time for a debate right now. We're at Eddie V's, about to have dinner with one of the partners and he just walked in."

"You at least need to hire security," I say, but it's too late. She hung up.

Frustrated, I consider calling my father in the morning, or even going to see him, but where will that get me? Nowhere besides putting more attention on my parents if I'm being watched. I rotate back into my comfy spot, eat my meal and when I'm done, I walk into the bathroom, dig in my purse, and pull out the napkin Rafael gave me. I carry it back to bed with me, lay it down next to my gun, and study the neat, controlled, masculine script. Control is a good word. I believe he's a man of great control. I have skills, he'd said. I'm curious about those skills, on a personal and professional level. Could I trust private security to protect the high-profile critical witnesses more than law enforcement? No, I think and settle back against the headboard, sipping my wine before googling "Walker Security," and what I find is impressive. Both reluctantly and with hope, as contradictory as those things sound, my "no" becomes a "maybe." Maybe, just maybe, Rafael is the answer to my problems.

I consider calling Blake Walker now, but it's later in New York than here. I need to sleep on this idea, and Lord help me, I'll have to convince Ed to pay for their services. That's not a task to attempt without doing my homework first. I add Blake's number to my phonebook in my cellphone and then do the same with Rafael's. I almost, so very almost, text him a thank you for walking me home.

But that's a bad idea. It's an invitation for another kiss I might crave, but do not dare allow myself, especially if we're about to be professionally attached. I clear my work to the empty side of the bed, the side that's always empty and needs to stay that way, turn out the light, and lay there staring at the ceiling, listening to every tiny sound. I need a dog, a big dog that knows how to cuddle me and kill an intruder. Of course, I'm never home, so that can't work. I settle my phone on my chest and force my eyes shut.

ADRIAN

It's on the north side of midnight and I'm at the dining room table Lucifer has set-up with the security feed, eating pizza with him and Adam, when Savage walks in, grabbing a seat next to me. "Deleon's a slippery bastard." He snatches up a slice of pizza. "I hate slippery bastards. Every lead Blake gave me came up dry."

"He's hunting," I say, tossing away the crust to my last slice, suddenly losing my appetite, "and he's a hell of a good hunter."

"Hunting *you*," Savage says. "Until a few days ago, you were in New York. How do we know he's not there, instead of here?"

"He's too smart to come to my territory," I say. "He wanted me to come to him."

"And here you are," Adam says. "Now what?"

A flash of Pri's pretty blue eyes drowning in fear flashes through my mind. "We need the list of witnesses. We follow that trail."

"What about Agent Pitt?" Savage asks, already reaching for another slice of pizza. "Ask him."

"The US Marshals handle witness protection," I say. "I need Pri to give us that list."

Adam arches a brow at me from across the table. "You're going to ask her for the list, Rafael?"

"What does his brother have to do with this?" Savage asks.

"He told her his name was Rafael," Lucifer offers.

"Oh shit," Savage murmurs. "She's going to be pissed when she finds out who you are."

"It was necessary," I say, tipping back my beer and taking a slug before I add, "I told her I'm with Walker. I told her we can help. If she calls, we know she's not only legit, but not being bribed or threatened to turn over witnesses to Deleon, which includes me."

"And if she doesn't call?" Adam asks.

"We figure out if she's dirty or in trouble, and act accordingly."

"Any chance Pitt has the list and you don't know it?" Lucifer asks.

"Doubtful," I say, pulling my phone from my pocket, "but worth trying." I punch in Pitt's autodial on speakerphone, because unlike anyone in my FBI days, at least my latter days, I trust these assholes. The question is, will they trust me when they discover all that went down with me and Waters?

Pitt answers on the second ring. "Hola," he answers. "What's cooking, man? You ready to come forward? Or at least meet the ADA?"

Considering Pri and I together make a bigger target, that's not something I'm willing to go on record with just yet. "I need to know who's on the witness list outside of me of course."

"I don't have that list," he says. "You know that. The DA's office is guarding the list, but there must not be anyone overly hot, or she wouldn't want you so damn badly. Come in. Meet her."

"Not yet," I say. "Get me the list and then we'll talk. Gotta run." I disconnect, thankful as fuck that Blake scrambles our phone location with whatever magic he works.

"You didn't tell him you're here," Adam says. "Interesting."

"He's dirty," Lucifer says. "I feel it straight to my fucking bones."

My mind is back on Pri and her distrust of law enforcement that clearly has a valid place in this story.

"Ditto," Savage says. "Pitt's dirty. I wonder if he's a bleeder. Wanna find out?"

"I do," Lucifer says. "I wanna find out."

"He's not dirty," I say. "He wants Waters to go down. He gave up years of his life setting him up, even if not as directly involved as I was."

"Does Blake know about him?" Adam asks simply, a man of few words, but what he says has a purpose.

"Of course he does," I say. "He's Blake."

As if Blake heard us speak his name, my cellphone rings with him on caller ID. I answer. "You're on speaker with all of us."

"Let's talk about Priscilla Miller, Adrian," he says.

He has my attention. "What about her?"

"I can never be a hundred percent certain, but I've spent the last hour checking and double-checking the research I'd done a few days ago. Her electronic fingerprint, including her bank accounts, read clean. I can't find any proof she's dirty, but—"

"Cash deals happen," I say. "It's the only way Waters deals. And he wouldn't leave a phone record. He's good, which is why we can't fuck up and let him get away." I glance around the room. "He's a monster, the likes of which we've rarely seen. He has to pay."

"And he will," Adam says.

"A-fucking-men," Lucifer murmurs.

"A-fucking-men," Savage agrees. "And we bury Deleon with him. Blake," he adds, "he's ghosting. I need more to grab him."

"I'm working on it," Blake assures him, shifting back to me, "Adrian, we need the witness protection list. I'm trying to pull strings, but we need Pri or the DA to give the okay. I say we give Pri twenty-four hours. If she doesn't come to us, I'll go to the DA and offer our services for free if that's what it takes."

For free.

For me.

"You don't have to do that," I say.

"You're one of us now," Blake says. "This is personal. Twenty-four hours. Do we agree?"

"Yes," I say, hoping like hell Pri makes that call to us on her own.

"Then we have a plan," Blake says. "What else?"

"Check out Agent Pitt," Savage chimes in.

I scowl his direction. "He's not dirty."

"I've given him a looksee," Blake confirms. "Nothing stands out."

I arch a brow at Savage who shrugs.

"Anything else?" Blake asks.

"Nothing." I say and when no one objections, Blake says, "More soon," and hangs up.

I stand and walk away from the crew, entering the kitchen to lean on the island, chin low.

"You okay?"

I glance up to find Adam on the other side of the island. "I was deep undercover. I lived it with Waters or I died."

"You think anyone here is naïve enough not to know that?"

"It changes how you look at a person, seeing what they can do."

"We all have our dirty laundry, man. You know that."

"Right," I say, but there is nothing right about where I let Waters drag me. I push off the island. "I'm going to get some shut-eye." I head toward the door and once I'm in my room alone, I sit down on the edge of the bed. The devil, the King Devil, is in the details, my details, and he means to drag me to hell with him. I should have killed him while I had the chance. At least two witnesses would still be alive.

WHEN HE'S DIRTY

Chapter Ten

ADRIAN

I'm up at 5 AM and dressed in gray sweats and a basic navy T-shirt, ready for a run. I exit my room and find the house quiet outside of Lucifer monitoring the security feed at the dining room table. "Coffee's ready," he says. "Savage covered me last night. He just went to catch some z's."

I nod and keep walking, entering the kitchen on a path to the back door only to find Adam, looking as ready for a run as I am, leaning on the counter with a cup in his hand. He sets it down and straightens. "You're running," he says. "I'm running."

"I'm in," Savage says, appearing in the kitchen as well.

"No," I say. "The three of us are going to draw way too much attention. Both of you go to bed."

"Fuck," Savage grumbles, scrubbing a jaw sporting a two-day stubble. "Right." He eyes Adam. "He's right. We're all so flipping hot and handsome, everyone will notice. And I'm as tired as an eighty-year-old grandma who baked a cake."

Adam grabs his cup. "I slept. You go sleep, Savage."

Savage, looking weary, doesn't argue. He rotates and I call after him, preparing him for what I know is coming, what's been weighing on me all night long.

"You'll have to kill Deleon to beat him, Savage. You get him first or he'll get you."

He half turns and winks. "I'm always first. And now to bed. I do my best killing with at least four hours." Savage disappears into the other room.

I eye Adam and his SEAL Team Six moral compass of gold. "Got anything to say about that?"

"Yeah," he says. "We running or not?"

In other words, we'll talk about our contrasting morals when it comes to murdering assholes later. Right now, this is his way of being here for me. And considering he's more of a silent type than a lecturing type, which works for me.

I give him a nod and we step outside into the sixty-something muggy morning, a perfect time to finish my workout before Pri heads out for hers. And she will. There is no question in my mind that Pri will take her ritual run this morning even if she most likely went to bed spooked and saying she wouldn't. It's a control thing, a need to feel as if the enemy can't take what is yours and familiar. The way a runner might use running to steady herself, to convince herself she's strong enough and brave enough to keep fighting a big bad wolf. I just hope like hell I can convince her I'm not the wolf.

Forty-five minutes later, Adam and I complete our run and we're out of sight, but present when Pri exits her house for her run. I feel this punch in my chest at the sight of her that I don't understand. Forcing my gaze from her long legs, I glance at Adam. "I need to be at the coffee shop when she gets there."

"I'll cover her," he says. "I've got her back. And yours. Go. Sweep her path forward. I'll follow her."

I nod, and take off, my mission to clear her a safe path.

By the time she's done with her run, I've left her with Adam's protection, and I'm in the coffee shop with my MacBook in front of me, sipping a coffee. And just as I expected, she walks in the door. And holy hell, I saw her running, but right now, seeing her here now, in pink shorts, her long athletic legs as bare as her make-up free face, she's so fucking beautiful. Obviously, I have a thing for her legs, but damn it, what is it with me and this woman? I've known my share of beauties, but none of them kept me awake at night thinking about them the way Pri does. None of them linger on my lips the way she does. I tell myself it's about the case, it has to be about the case. We're connected in a common cause. We're connected by the King Devil and there is no way that ends well.

She must feel me watching her because her gaze lifts and turns in my direction, and when her eyes fall on me, there is a rush of awareness between us, followed by white-hot lust, at least on my part. And despite how hands-off she should be, and is, I welcome it. Lust I can handle. Lust is familiar.

She gives me a tiny wave and a smile before she places her order, and damn it, there's a kick in my gut, something more than lust again. It's not familiar. It's not comfortable and I don't have time to find a way to dismiss it, either.

It's not long before she slides into the seat across from me. "Morning," she says, her voice so fucking sweet, a beautiful contradiction of tough and charming.

"Good morning," I say, and she is even prettier this close.

She motions to my cup. "White mocha or butterscotch?"

"White mocha," I confirm. "I have a sweet tooth." I point out the bag of M & M's on the table. "Breakfast of champions. Want some?"

She laughs. "For breakfast? No, but have you tried the new brownie ones?"

"I'm more of a traditional guy."

"The brownie M & M's will convert you, I promise." Her cellphone rings and she pulls it from the running belt around her waist, eyeing the number, her mood sobering instantly. "Defense's lead counsel. Maybe I do need chocolate for breakfast. Sorry. I have to take this." She answers the line and says, "A little early to get a call from you, Daniel. You want to make a deal, right?"

Her name is called out and she stands and walks to the counter. Grabbing her coffee, she heads back in my direction but pauses halfway between the coffee bar and the table.

But I am still close, the only person in hearing distance and only barely, but I manage to pick up pieces of the conversation. "Then maybe you should tell your client to stop hurting people," she says her voice low, taut, then she says, "What bigger fish?"

She turns slightly and the sound barrier broadens. That's all I get before she ends the call. By the time she's returned, I've packed up my bag. "I need to go," she says. "Unfortunately, I have to get to the office sooner than expected."

I stand, studying her, searching her lovely face, and finding tension ticking along her jawline. "Tell me you didn't agree to a deal."

"You heard," she assumes.

"Enough," I say. "Tell me you didn't accept a deal," I repeat.

"No," she says, "but he wants me to meet with him and Waters. Waters is offering me a bigger fish."

"Who?"

"I can't tell you that."

Now my jaw is ticking. "He's too dangerous to let get away, and too many people gave up their lives to get him where he is now, for you to set him free."

"I'm not going to just set him free. I want him behind bars. And how do you know anything about this case?"

"I know," I say. "Who does he want to trade?"

"I can't—"

"*Who,* Pri?" I insist.

"I can't tell you that."

"Whoever it is, isn't as bad as Waters."

"You can't know that."

"And yet, I do." I catch the fingers of her hand with mine and I don't miss her tiny intake of breath or the fact that she doesn't pull away. "Call Blake Walker. He'll stop the bloodshed. He'll help you win this case."

"I can't even guarantee I can get his fees approved."

"Walker will do this for free if they have to."

She blinks up at me. "Free? Why would they do that?"

"Because I'm involved and because Waters really *is* the King Devil. Waters will keep hurting people. Don't let that happen." My hand falls from hers. "I'm going to leave, at least for now, and let you think."

I step around her and take two steps when she calls out. "Wait!"

I half turn and she asks, "How do you know all of this? *How?*"

"Call Blake." I rotate again and this time I really do leave.

PRI

I stare after Rafael, confused about whose side he's on. It feels like he's on mine, but he knows too much about Waters to be some random guy in a coffee shop I just happened to meet. He could be working for Waters, playing games with me. Or Rafael could be Adrian Mack. It's a crazy thought. Of course, undercover work is his thing but no, it can't be true. It's not true. And yet, it popped into my head. When things pop into my head, they usually matter. Oh God. Why am I standing here? I just let him leave.

I race after him and exit the coffee shop, scanning left and right, but he's nowhere to be found.

Chapter Eleven

PRI

Still in front of the coffee shop, I grab my phone and dial Rafael's number, but after several rings it goes to voicemail. "It's Pri," I say. "Please call me." I hang up and start walking. He wants me to call Blake Walker. I'll call him, but I need to do it at home, alone.

Hurrying forward, I replay every word I've exchanged with Rafael, trying to find clues, but I'm back to square one. I'm even trying to convince myself our paths crossing was just luck.

I enter my house and it's frustrating to feel that I need to search it before I can even make the call. I grab my gun from the hall table where I left it before my run and do my search. When I'm done, I sit down on my bed and try Rafael again. I reach his voicemail again, and this concerns me. I thought we had a connection. I thought there was something between us. *Call Blake*, he'd said several times. I immediately punch in Blake Walker's number.

"Priscilla Miller," he answers. "Blake Walker. Rafael told me you'd be calling."

"How did you know it was me?" I ask. "I didn't give Rafael my number."

"I'm good at finding out things. I'm sending you a text with a private Dropbox with references. There are some powerful people on the list, including a few inside the White House. Feel free to call them."

"Can you include a fee list?"

"We're not cheap," Blake says. "But can the DA afford to lose the case or make a lesser deal in an election year?"

"The trial isn't going be over in time for the election anyway."

"The case may be if you let him walk."

"Rafael told you he wants to make a deal."

"Yes," he says. "He did."

"Rafael says he's here on a job for Walker?"

"Everything he does is with Walker. We're family. And we don't get bribed or turned by the likes of Waters. We also don't get scared. You need to act now before someone else dies."

"I know that."

"Before you make a deal, at least meet with one of my men."

"Isn't that what I did with Rafael?"

"I'd like to send Adam to meet with you at the office."

"And Rafael?"

"Will step back in at the appropriate moment, but Rafael said I was to be a reference for him with you. I'm offering that to you in Adam. Ask him about Rafael."

"What about you?" I ask. "What do you think of Rafael?"

"I only employ men I trust, men that I know will always come through. Rafael would take a fall to save anyone on this team. And we would do the same for him."

"This case is personal to him, isn't it?"

"That's between you and him."

"I know who he is."

"A hero, Ms. Miller. He's a hero. What time can I send Adam over to meet with you?"

"Two o'clock."

"Two it is. What can I do for you before we hang up?"

"I need to speak with Adrian Mack."

He's silent a moment, before he says, "I'll see what I can do." He disconnects.

I grab my MacBook and pull up the references Blake has sent me and I'm blown away. The Secretary of State is on the list. *The Secretary of State!* There's a number inviting me to call him. It's way too early to make that call, but I'm already won over. We need Walker Security on this case. And as for *Rafael*—I don't know if he's Rafael or Adrian, but I hope like heck I didn't make-out in a bathroom with our key witness. And really, truly, it would be the definition of my screwed-up love life if I did. My lashes lower and I think about him catching my fingers this morning. I'd felt that touch all over. I'd felt connected to him. My lashes lift. If he's Adrian, was anything that happened between us even real?

Maybe he learned a little too much about games from the King Devil himself.

━━━━━━━━━ ⟨∞⟩ ━━━━━━━━━

ADRIAN

I ignore her calls.

I have no option. She's the one with options now. What I do next depends on what she does next.

Once Blake has a fresh heads up about Pri, I shower and dress in jeans and boots, heading to the kitchen to fill a cup with steaming coffee.

"What's your feeling on this?" Adam asks, joining me, also freshly showered, his sweats exchanged for jeans and a "SEALs do it better" T-shirt meant to be a jab at Savage, who started his career in the Special Forces. That he ended up an assassin for our own government is not a pleasant subject, unless, for instance, you want him to kill someone like Deleon.

"I don't know," I say grimly. "I just don't know, but I hope like hell she calls Blake."

Once his cup is steaming, we take up opposite sides of the island and he says, "I'm not sure her calling or not calling tells you what you want to know, man. Sounds to me like she doesn't trust anyone."

My cellphone rings and I pull it from my pocket to find Blake on the caller ID. I show it to Adam and then answer on speaker. "You have me and Adam here, Blake."

"Fucking perfect," Blake says. "Just the two assholes I need. Adrian, she called. I gave her references. And as we agreed, I set-up Adam to meet her at two o'clock at the DA's office to remove your risk of being recognized."

"How do you feel about the call?" I ask.

"It was as expected," he replies. "No red flags. She asked about Rafael. I think she suspects that you're not who you say you are."

"Yeah," I say. "Me, too, but for now she isn't sure and I need it to stay that way."

"I'll leave that to you to handle," Blake says. "You're the one on a hitlist. The bottom line is that it looks like one way or the other, we'll get official placement on the case and that allows us to work more effectively."

79

"Thanks, Blake," I say. "I hope that happens."

"It will," he says and then, proving me right in my claim to Pri earlier, he adds, "Even if we have to volunteer our services. More soon." He disconnects and I lower my chin to my chest, relieved that Pri called Blake, and if I'm honest, it runs deeper than my duty to take down Waters.

"You're into this woman, aren't you?" Adam asks. "She got to you."

I glance up at him. "Yeah," I admit because fuck me, it's obvious, "and I can't figure out what the fuck she's doing to me," I add. "I'm like a freaking slinky slinking down the stairs and having the wires get all wonky. It has to be the case. It's personal to me and her."

"Or not. I've seen how you are with women. You don't get wonky. *Ever*."

"I'm a hypocrite for bringing this up," I say, bringing up a nagging worry, "and I say hypocrite, considering some of the things you don't want to know I've done in my life, but she defended some really bad people at her father's firm."

"And got out. That matters."

He's right, but I know from experience that swimming with the sharks doesn't just make you bleed, it changes you. It had to have changed her. "Just be aware."

"All right then. Good thing I'm going to meet with her. I'm a good read, man. I'll tell you if I'm worried."

He is a good read, I've seen that first hand, but he doesn't read me, he doesn't know who I became with Waters. Which means he might not be able to read Pri. And yet, I would. Surely I would. Unless her getting to me has clouded my judgment.

"What comes next, man?" Adam asks. "Walker joins the prosecution team. Do you come forward?"

"Not until the last possible minute."

"You have to tell Pri," he says. "You know you have to tell Pri."

"Go to the meeting," I say. "I'll decide what comes next after that meeting."

He doesn't push. He gets it. As Blake said, I'm on a hitlist and one wrong move could expose me and land me six feet under. I can't let Pri, intentionally or not, put me there. I can't end Waters or protect her from him if I'm dead.

Chapter Twelve

PRI

My father always says that a red tie is a power tie, it's a statement about money, power, and success. My father possesses all of those things so I tend to take him at his word. Not that money and power motivate me, but success does. I want the best me representing those who cannot represent themselves. My father also says that if you don't have money, power, and success, the perception that you do will influence others around you.

I might have left his lifestyle and motivations behind, but I learned and learned well from him with my own twist of morality, and in today's case, style. I dress in a black skirt and jacket but choose a red silk shell to complement the solid color. I'm not against a power pantsuit for a woman, but for me, a skirt reads and feels more feminine and I happen to think it works for me, not against me.

Whatever the case, ready to take on the world—or perhaps the underworld is more appropriate—I slide into the back of an Uber which is easier than finding parking for my own car downtown. Normally, I'd walk to work, but that option feels better avoided outside my small, safe neighborhood, filled with active nosy neighbors. Exactly why the gun in my purse and the

Secretary of State's phone number in my possession lend me confidence in where the future is headed. I'm protecting me. Perhaps the Walker Security references will convince me that they can protect our witnesses. And maybe, just maybe, those of us still living can survive.

I arrive at work and manage to dodge all the obstacles, including people, questions, gossip, and a bullpen of desks, between me and my office. Once I'm there, I shut my door, settle behind my desk and stick my purse in my drawer. Once my briefcase is unpacked, I eagerly start calling the Walker references. I start with a few private sector contacts and everyone eagerly takes my call, raving about Walker, Blake, and his brothers. Adam and someone named Savage are mentioned as well. When I finally dial the Secretary of State, I end up talking to his secretary, who says she's been told to tell me that "Blake Walker is the best man I know and please tell him I said so." That call wins me over. I'm sold on Walker and the idea that Rafael works for Blake has me thinking he's probably really just Rafael, not Adrian. Either way, I'm about to go hunt down Ed when there's a knock on my door before Grace pops her head inside my office.

I motion her forward and she hurries toward me, looking pretty in a pink suit dress, her skin glowing.

"When can we talk about Josh?" she asks, perching on the arm of one of my visitor chairs.

"If you love him, after this case," I say. "If he broke your heart, I'll go beat him up while I'm in war mode."

"I'm worried about you," Grace says. "I know it's not likely, but what if Waters comes after you?"

"I'm worried about my witnesses. Law enforcement thinks the killer is one of Waters' top men, but they don't know. They're operating on speculation."

"I'm worried about you," she repeats.

"I'm fine. You know they'd just replace me if I died. Waters won't come after me and he's isolated right now. He can't communicate with anyone."

"Maybe his attorney is dirty. And if you die, the case will be delayed and who knows what would happen. It would get crazier than it already is now. What about Ed?" she asks, softening her voice. "Is he worried?"

"He's worried about everything to do with this case. He's a beast right now."

"I mean about himself. I mean, yes, you can be replaced, but if he was suddenly out of the picture, the case would stall. I wonder if a new DA would even have the courage to go forward with it at all."

"Let's not put that into the universe," I say, and yet, she's right, I think. Lord help me, the collective hell, might just motivate Ed to make a deal.

"It's not about the universe," she snips. "You need to take the threats seriously. Waters has proven to be the devil he calls himself. I don't know how you ended up on this case. Okay, I do," she quickly amends. "You learned how these monsters think when you were with your father. Listen to your gut and listen."

I learned with my father.

And there it is. My reputation for defending monsters. It's a part of me, but damn it, maybe winning this case will make people forget. Maybe it will make me forget.

Agent Pitt appears in my doorway. "Got a minute?" he asks.

Grace glances over her shoulder at him and then back at me. "I can wait." She pushes to her feet. "Can you do lunch?"

"Not until this is over for every reason you just gave me to set that timeline."

"Drinks it is," she says. "I'll call you later."

She backs out of the doorway and Agent Pitt walks into my office. No. He doesn't just walk in, he shuts the door with him inside, a puff of cranky energy hitched on his back for the ride. "I heard Waters is trying to make a deal."

My brows knit together. "Heard from who?"

"Why haven't you told me?"

"Heard from *who*?" I repeat, my voice a hard push this time.

He waves that off. "His attorney is buzzing it around to anyone who'll listen."

"Of course," I say dryly, really not that surprised by this realization as I add, "He wants the DA to be pressured to take the deal."

"What did he offer?"

"A guy named Jason Whitaker. He's an attorney long suspected of helping some very powerful people launder money or just plain hide it."

"I know him. What's your play?"

I have no idea why I hold back my intentions to stay my course, but I do without hesitation. "I'll let you know when I know."

"What does that mean?" he grumbles.

"It means," I gather up the Walker references on my desk and stand, "that I need to see the DA before I make any decisions. I am, after all, an Assistant District Attorney, not *the* District Attorney." I round my desk and he doesn't move. Pitt's a big man, broad and fit, his hair and eyes as dark as his mood, and yes, now I notice that he is rather good looking. And yet, even standing close to him, there is no buzz to my skin or heat in my belly. We don't vibe romantically at all. Right now, he's just a wall blocking my path.

"What is it you want from me, Agent Pitt?" I snap.

"A lot of people worked really hard to take down Waters," he bites out.

Rafael's words come back to me: *too many people gave up their lives to get him where he is now for you to set him free.* Which in hindsight was a big statement. My decision is made. No deal, not if I can stop it from happening. I won't set Waters free.

"Pri," Pitt snaps, the use of my first name, not under objection, as it's my preference, but his impatient tone is another story.

I blink him back into view. "I know many people worked and sacrificed to arrest Waters, Agent Pitt. I get it. You know I do."

"You sure about that?" he presses. "Bodies are dropping. Maybe you don't have the stomach for it."

"I never have the stomach for murder," I say.

"Maybe that's why Waters thinks you'll make a deal. You've made plenty in the past for guys like him."

"Don't push me, Agent Pitt."

I try to step around him and he moves with me, blocking my path again. "Are you going to make the deal?"

My heart is now thundering in my chest. "Move out of my way," I order, my voice low, tight, controlled when my pulse is not.

The intercom on my desk buzzes and Ed's voice bellows. "I understand you have something to tell me, Ms. Miller. Why are you not in my office telling me now?"

I walk to the desk and punch the button to reply with "Because Agent Pitt is discussing the case with me. I'm on my way."

"Make it now," he snaps and the line goes dead.

"The defense is manipulating you," Pitt accuses.

I step back in front of him. "Why don't you do something besides trying and failing to intimidate me and help, Agent Pitt? Adrian Mack changes everything. Tell him it's time for a one-on-one talk. *Now*." I step around him and this time he doesn't stop me. I open the door and exit to the hallway, leaving one hotheaded male opinion, and on my way for another.

I start down the hallway and Cindy steps into pace with me. "Tell me you're not making a deal."

I glance over at her and grimace. "My God, did the defense do a press release on the offer?"

"Might as well have," she says, "it's buzzing everywhere. What are you going to do?"

"Send Waters to jail for the rest of his life." We halt at the alcove that houses Ed's office, and I peek inside relieved that his prickly secretary Lynn is missing. "Wish me luck."

She squeezes my arm and doesn't let go. "People are dying."

"And they'll keep dying for years to come as long as Waters has the resources and opportunity to kill them." I pull out of her reach and enter Ed's office.

I find him standing with his back to me at his window. "Ed?"

He rotates and motions to the door, his expression taut, his tie red, of course, which tells me a story I already know about Ed. He's a man who needs power and presently fears losing it. He's an asshole, impatient and demanding. He's also a man of courage to even take us down this path with Waters. He cares about justice. He motions to the door. "Shut it."

I do as he orders and he says, "Tell me you have Adrian Mack because if we lose Waters and don't take the trade, I'm fucked."

I walk to a visitor's chair and capture the back with my hands. "Waters is manipulating you. The trial is not going to end until after the election and he knows it. Stay the course."

He scrubs his jaw and settles his hands under his jacket on his waist. "And if our witnesses keep falling and Waters pulls the trade?"

A memory of Rafael holding my hand and telling me to call Walker Security plays in my mind and lends confidence to my next statement. "First of all," I say, "my gut is that Adrian Mack will show up, but not until right before the trial. Maybe even after it starts." He opens his mouth to, no doubt, tell me that's not good enough and I hold up a hand. "We need to hire private security to protect the witnesses."

"Give me a break, Miller. They're as corruptible as the next guy."

"I recommend we make an educated gamble on Walker Security," I say. "I talked with them. I've checked references, including one from the Secretary of State today and yes, that's *the* Secretary of State, among others." I set the file in my hand on his desk. "They won't be cheap, but this is about putting Waters behind bars and keeping you, the man behind his demise, in office. As a bonus, I feel like hiring them will make Mack more comfortable coming forward."

"How much?"

"I don't have the numbers yet," say, "but how much are justice and your career worth?"

"Your career is on the line here, too. We're riding the same boat. A hole sinks us both. You get that right?"

"Yes. I get it. Hire Walker Security. They're based out of New York, but they have a team in the city for another case and can start now."

"How did you find them?"

"Are you really going to micromanage me right now, Ed? The Secretary of State recommended them. I know it's not the President but—"

He holds up a hand. "Fine. Hire them. I'll call the US Marshals' office and make it official."

"Don't call them until I talk to Walker this afternoon. I don't want to risk one of those leaks that sinks us."

"All right."

"And I think you need them to protect you, too, Ed. If Waters gets desperate, there's no telling what he'll do."

"I'm single, I'm ex-military, and I'm capable of protecting myself. Use the resources for other people." He motions me onward. "Go. Make it happen."

I hesitate. I want to push him to accept protection, but I'll take what I can get for now. I exit his office and in this moment, I feel relief and a sense of calm that defies the situation. And I know why. It means Rafael is involved. My reaction has to mean I trust him. Unless this crazy attraction I have to him has clouded my judgment? In which case, more than my career will die. I might go with it.

Chapter Thirteen

PRI

By the time I'm in my office, Blake has emailed me contracts, non-disclosures, and other documents. I'm ready to hand over the witnesses to Walker. And right on time, Adam arrives.

Adam turns out to be tall, very tall, like six-four or five, good looking, with dark wavy hair and blue eyes. We sit down at my two-person conference table and I'm struck by his calm energy.

"Why didn't Rafael come with you?" I ask.

He levels me in a stare. "I think you know why."

It's a tricky reply. It could be about the kiss or Rafael's identity. "I'd feel better if he were here."

"I'm a good second choice. I was a Navy SEAL, on Team Six. My specialty is disguises. I'm good at being present and not seen."

"But you're so—well—"

He arches a brow. "Big?"

"Yes."

He leans closer. "If I can hide, I can hide your witnesses. Everything happening right now is about protecting them and protecting you."

"Everything?"

"*Everything*," he repeats.

"I guess that's a topic I can argue with *Rafael*."

His expression doesn't change, but I swear his lips hint at a curve. "You and *Rafael* do have plenty to discuss. I'm sure you can appreciate the position your relationship places on his duty."

I could read his statement a few ways and he knows it. I leave it alone for now, and go over the case, focusing on the safety of our witnesses.

"As it should be. Who have you told about us?"

"Just the DA."

"Good. We'll handle the US Marshals at the highest level and discreetly. Our plan is to make it seem as if those witnesses are still in place," he explains. "We'll place our people in their positions. If Deleon comes for them, we'll get him."

"You know about Deleon?"

"We don't take a case we don't research first. We believe he's the one killing your witnesses and we're looking for him. If we get Deleon, I suspect he'll sing to save himself."

"If we get him," I say, "nothing he can say will convince me to save him. I need Adrian Mack."

"And I feel certain he'll show up in time for your trial."

"And why exactly do you feel certain of such a thing?"

"Because you called Walker Security." He stands up. "Let us get to work before Deleon beats us to another witness." I blink and he's gone.

The way I blinked and Rafael was gone this morning.

I can only hope that means Adrian will soon appear.

For now, I return to my desk and get to work.

With Walker on board, my confidence in the case against Waters is restored. I dig into damage control for lost witnesses and try to find ways to save those portions of the prosecution. That turns into hours and hours with my team, pinning down our options. As the afternoon becomes the evening, Cindy and I end up at the coffee shop again. And yes, I secretly hope Rafael will show up, but he doesn't, even after Cindy departs.

When finally I gather my work to head home, I decide it's silly to take an Uber for three blocks. Then I decide it's stupid not to because I stupidly didn't talk to Adam about my own safety. I take the Uber. I tip well. I stand outside my door and hesitate. If my witnesses are protected, is killing me the fastest way to end the case, or at least delay it until next year? I unzip my purse and remove my gun before keying in my security code. It buzzes and I open the door, listening a moment to not much of anything before I flip on the light. Still nervous—I've clearly psyched myself out—I shut the door, lock it and then lean on the hard surface, listening to nothing again.

It's moments like this, alone and scared, that I question my career choices, but the fear works two ways. It reminds me that every victim that I've ever defended most likely felt fear. It reminds me that I defended some of the people that caused that fear and I owe a debt to society in the aftermath.

Inhaling, I force myself to get this over with, to clear the way to a glass of wine and calmness by finishing my search of the house. I walk to the living room and I see a shadow in the darkness and I feel another person in the room. I flip on the light only to gasp. Rafael is sitting on the oversized chair facing me.

WHEN HE'S DIRTY

Chapter Fourteen

PRI

I aim my gun at the man who told me his name was Rafael. "You're Adrian Mack."

"Yes," he says. "Rafael is my brother."

"As in the singer?"

"Yes. He uses our mother's maiden name. His name felt as close to honest as I dared."

"Really? Nothing about what you did with me was honest."

"There's a price on my head," he says. "That's as real as it gets and it has to dictate my actions."

"Therefore you *had* to kiss me? And make me look and feel like an idiot?"

He stands up, all kinds of gorgeous, and I shouldn't be noticing, not now. What is wrong with me with this man?

"Nothing between us besides a meeting was planned, Pri. It just happened and things don't just happen to me. You want to lower that gun?"

I don't even think about lowering my weapon. "How do I know you're not working for Waters? Maybe you're the one who's killing my witnesses."

"I could have killed you several times over. I think you know that."

His voice is low, calm. Mine is not. It's slightly higher than normal, while my pulse is rapid, irritating me with the distracting pitter-patter in my chest. "I didn't take the trade Waters offered and give him a deal," I inform him. "Maybe that changed things."

"Why would I play with you like that?"

"Why did Waters ever play with anyone?" I counter.

"Because he's a sadistic bastard. I'm not. I even brought champagne."

I blink with this odd announcement and follow the lift of his chin to the coffee table. "Why would you break into my house and bring champagne? What *is this*?"

"A way for us to toast to taking down Waters, you and me—we'll get him."

I want to trust him. I want to believe him, but I have to come to that decision safely. I already know I'm susceptible to him, perhaps dangerously so. I can't do this alone with him. I take a step and grab my phone from the hall table where I'd set it automatically when I'd entered the house. "If you're honest, you won't mind if Agent Pitt joins us."

I don't know how he moves so fast, but by the time I pull up my phonebook, he's in front of me. Another blink and he has my gun and phone, and I'm pressed against the living room wall, masculine spice teasing my nostrils, hard muscles pressed to my body. Our eyes meet, a battle of wills melding with anger and heat, as well as fear, that is frighteningly arousing.

What is wrong with me?

Rebelliously, my chin lifts. "Is this where you kill me?"

A low sound escapes his lips, and he shifts, his hands and legs that were touching me are gone, his fists pressed to the wall by my head, his arms and body caging me by simple proximity. It's a confusing thing to

95

be trapped and yet untouched. As if he's reading my mind, he says, "I *am trying* not to bully you or scare you, woman, but damn it, do you want to get us both killed?" His voice is low, taut, with a rasp of what might be anger in the deep baritone.

"Pitt is one of the good guys," I hiss.

"I can't afford to trust anyone," he says. "I wouldn't be here now if we hadn't gotten personal, but I felt I owed you this and it's easier for Walker to operate if you're in the know on who I am."

"Pitt says he's your friend."

"No one outside of Walker is my friend."

"You worked the case with him," I argue. "He's passionate about keeping Waters behind bars."

"We don't know who's watching Pitt or listening in on his calls. And you and I together make a hell of a giant target."

"You think I'm a target?"

"Anyone in Waters' path is a target and will remain so every day he's alive. The biggest mistake of my life was not killing him every time I had the chance. And I'll say that on the stand under oath." He pushes off the wall but he remains directly in front of me. "I have to be a last-minute surprise witness. And I want immunity."

"Why would you need immunity? You were undercover."

"I want fucking immunity. And now," he adds, "I'm going to go drink the expensive-ass champagne I brought and already opened. Shoot me if you want to, but don't call Pitt." He starts to walk away.

I catch his arm and the muscle there flexes beneath my touch, his gaze colliding with mine, and the rush of awareness between us is scorching. It's also comforting. This is real. This is not something he could fake. "Why would you need immunity?" I press again. "You were undercover."

Tension ticks in his jaw. "That's the deal. My testimony for immunity. And if you keep touching me, I'm going to forget why I shouldn't have touched you."

I don't let him go. It's as if some part of me is sure he will disappear and that same part of me wants him to touch me again, to kiss me again. "I hate that you lied to me."

He rotates back toward me, somehow now just a little closer. I can smell his cologne stronger now, and I decide it's an alluring mix of vanilla and spice, man and beast. "I had to meet you," he says. "I had to know I trusted you."

"And do you?"

"More than you do me right now. You're still touching me, Pri."

"I'm afraid you're going to disappear. I'm not letting go."

It's an invitation I don't mean to deliver—or maybe I do because I swear my entire body sighs as his fingers tunnel into my hair and he steps into me, his powerful body pressed to mine. "Right now, you're giving me plenty of reasons to stay." His mouth lowers, a breath from mine. "Right now, all I want is another taste of you."

"I thought you weren't going to kiss me again until I trust you?" I challenge softly, already breathless.

"Maybe if I kiss you enough, and in the right places, you will." His mouth closes down on mine and there's this blast of passion in the long kiss that follows, in the lick of our tongues, as if we're breathing each other in. His hand finds my lower back and he molds me closer, inhaling and parting our lips. "Tell me to stop and I will."

"I should," I whisper.

"I should, too," he murmurs, "but I don't want to."

"This doesn't mean I trust you," I vow.

His grip in my hair tightens, an erotic tug and he pulls my head back, my gaze to his. "Good. That will keep you alive."

I'm not sure if that's a warning about himself or Waters, and I don't seem to care, not when his mouth is on my mouth again. Not when his hand slides over my backside and he arches my hips against his hips, the thick ridge of his erection pressing into my belly. It's insane, even reckless, when I am not reckless, how much I want Adrian inside me right now, desperately, so very desperately.

I moan and my fingers close around his T-shirt, my tongue meeting his tongue with almost desperate strokes. It's been so long since I've been with a man, so very long since I even wanted a man, and now, all I know is want and need. And my god, the man can kiss. I am swimming in sensation, clinging to him, and his hands are now all over me and I want them all over me.

He tears his mouth from mine and stares down at me, his stare probing, but I don't look away. I let him see me, really see me, in hopes that he will find what he needs to trust me, too. This is a two-way street, I'm just not there yet. I'm not ready to show him who I am, who I really am. And I have a feeling I will never really know Adrian Mack. And therein lies just one of my problems.

I don't know Adrian. I don't even come close to knowing him, and yet, I'm alone with him, vulnerable when he kisses me. Vulnerable when he touches me. And vulnerable is something I never wanted to be in my personal or professional life ever again.

And yet here I am.

Vulnerable.

Naked in nearly every way.

Exposed.

Perhaps even in danger, and yet, I just can't seem to care.

His gaze lowers to my lips and down over my breasts and I don't even know how the buttons of the red silk are undone, my breasts heaving against the black lace of my bra. He moans, this low, rough rumble and his gaze lifts to mine. "You're beautiful, Pri, and nothing that I expected."

I don't know what that means and so I whisper, "And you are not Rafael."

He doesn't laugh. "Adrian," he says. "I'm Adrian, and I'm going to make you remember me when I'm gone."

Unbidden, the promised goodbye in those words punches me in the gut and I tell myself it's about the case, but then he's kissing me again. And there is something oh so dirty about this kiss. I have never experienced such a thing, not like this, when his tongue all but promises he will do naughty things to me and I will like every single one. My hands are on his chest, fingers flexing and then curling, while I lean into the long hard lines of his powerful body. Another rough, masculine moan slides from his throat before his mouth is gone, and I'm panting with the need for its return.

But already he's turned me toward the door, and he's tugging my jacket down my shoulders, holding it at my wrists as he leans in, his breath warm at my ear. He hesitates and I can feel the pulse of his arousal mix with mine. There is a dominance in Adrian that should scare me for more than one reason, because of my past with another man and then, of course, the fact, of who he is. I don't know if I can trust him. And Lord help me, that is almost arousing. No. There is no *almost* to it. Seconds tick by laden with desire—his and mine. My nipples pucker, my sex clenches in anticipation.

I can almost taste some erotic demands on his lips that never come. He yanks away the jacket and tosses it aside, turning me back around to face him, his eyes meeting mine. He searches my face again, and I don't know what he's looking for, but he says, "Obviously, I haven't kissed you enough."

His mouth crashes down on mine and I'm done fighting this. I don't have it in me. I don't want to even try. My hands slide under his shirt, hot, taut skin over hard muscle, and he responds by tearing his shirt over his head and tossing it aside. I have a few blinks to appreciate a sculpted torso, black and red-inked arms, and a tapered waist, before he's kissing me again, tugging my skirt up my hips, and just that fast, his mouth is gone and he's already on one knee in front of me. My skirt is gathered at my waist, and he catches the strings of my panties in his fingers and tugs the silk down my body. I untangle one foot and forget the other. His lips are on my belly—God, *his lips are on my belly*—and I'm trembling. I am so aroused, I'm weak in the knees.

His lips travel lower and anticipation thrums through me. I want him lower. I want him in the most intimate part of me, but just as I'm fading into that place of no return, a horrible thought jolts me. I lean forward and press my hands to his shoulders. "Wait. My God, is this one of Waters' evil games? Are you going to get me two seconds from orgasm and kill me?"

His lashes lower, his head tilting down, hair teasing the naked skin of my belly before he's on his feet, his hand under my hair on my neck, tilting my gaze to his.

"This is not a game and I will never hurt you. No matter what. I need you to remember that."

"How do I know you're telling the truth?"

"I guess you'll just have to live through your orgasm."

Heat rushes to my cheek and I actually laugh. "I can't believe we're having this conversation."

"Trust is a two-way street, sweetheart. You need to remember that."

"And what if we never trust each other?"

"Well then, I guess we can just fuck our way through the trial. And then fuck some more to celebrate that bastard never seeing sunlight again. Unless you'd rather not. It's your decision, Pri."

Chapter Fifteen

ADRIAN

Pri's lips part at my bold words. "You think this is that simple?" she challenges. "We just fuck our way through the trial?"

"It's not even close to that simple," I say, not at all surprised at how much I mean that statement. Nothing about how I react to this woman is simple. Nothing about running from the King Devil is simple, which is why running isn't what I have in mind. But right now, she's all I have on my mind. She's all I can seem to make matter. "But that doesn't mean we shouldn't do it," I say.

The very fact that Waters would agree to that statement, and that I know him that well, grinds through me, and yet I say exactly what he would yet again. "It's all about living in the moment, not the fear." Cursing myself, and all the parts of me that will never be the same after the Devils, I have to force myself to release her, to press my hands to the wall and not her body. "Or not. If you don't want me to touch you, I won't touch you. And you have no idea how much effort it just took for me to stop touching you."

She blinks her long, dark lashes and looks up at me with intelligent doe eyes, laden with heat and desire, and I am downright vibrating with the need to reach for her. "Ethically I have to tell the judge we're involved."

"Are you asking me if I care?"

"Yes."

"You do what you need to do. You're good enough to sell the judge on you and on why we came together."

"Which is why?"

"People are dying and we're surviving, sweetheart." I pause. "Together, Pri."

She studies me for several long beats and then she shocks me by tugging her blouse over her head and tossing it away. By the time it's hit the ground, we've come together again, a collision of passion, bodies pressed close, my hand on her head while our lips press together, tongues dancing. My fingers work the front clasp of her bra and I tear my mouth from hers to drag the straps over her shoulders. I let it fall and my gaze rakes over the swell of her full breasts, the sleek pucker of her plump nipples.

I tweak one perfect peak with my finger and watch the pleasure slide over her face before I lean in to kiss her neck, whispering at her ear, "There is nothing wrong with fucking. Nothing at all."

Her hand is on my face and while she doesn't respond, I'm speaking to what I've sensed in her, what I feel when I'm around her. She, unlike me, is not a natural rule-breaker. She's wound tight, always in control. Always just a little bit afraid of what happens if she is not. I stopped caring at some point, and for just a while, it was a façade of perfection. Realization hits me and I pull back to stare down at her, aware now of what draws us together. She needs a little taste of safe rebellion and I need a little taste of something good, *someone* good. I need her and yet all I say is, "It's okay to be bad with me. Just with me."

"Just with you?"

"Yes," I say, and while I'm talking about the case, I'm also talking about sex. There is also something unfamiliar but distinctly possessive in the words, in what I feel for Pri. "Just with me." I kiss her hard and fast and my lips curve. "Let's find out if you live to see orgasm number two."

She blushes a pretty pink, and Jesus, she's so freaking beautiful, her expression soft and laden with desire . Holy hell, I want to take Pri to a place of pleasure and escape, though I know it's a mistake. But then, I'm the devil's spawn and she smells like Texas sunshine and flowers, two things I've known too little of as of late.

I tug down her skirt and unzip it, sliding it down her hips. I go to my knee and help her get rid of it and her panties. And then I'm back right where I want to be, right where she wanted me before she decided an orgasm was a prelude to me killing her.

I kiss her belly, fingers sliding between her slick thighs, then pressing inside her. Her soft moan and arched hips stiffen my cock, and if she were anyone else, I'd be inside her right now, thinking about me, not her. That's how selfish the devil's made me, how self-centered. But back then, I wanted everything with anybody to just serve a purpose and be over, usually forever, nice and simple, but as I've already realized, nothing about her is simple. Nothing about me with Pri is simple.

For the first time in a very long time, I want another's pleasure far more than I want my own. I lean in and lick her clit. She sucks in a breath and my lips curve. Holy hell, I don't know the last time I smiled during sex, but Little Miss Pri is a first in all kinds of ways. I know better than to fuck who I protect and I am protecting her. I slide my hand down her bare leg and lift it to my shoulder, my hand on her backside, cupping it and fitting her snugly against me. I suckle her, lick her, explore her with my fingers, my tongue, my mouth, and too damn soon as far as I'm concerned, she's gasping as her body spasms around my fingers. I ease her through it with slower licks and when her knee starts to give out, I catch her around the waist, holding her up, lowering her leg.

I'm staring up at her, her hands on my shoulders, her eyes all satisfied and awed, when she says, "It's been a long time since—I haven't—"

I'm hanging on that sentence for reasons I can't explain when the doorbell rings and my cellphone starts buzzing. I'm grabbing her clothes and on my feet handing them to her in about two seconds. "Expecting someone?" I ask softly.

"No," she whispers. "No one."

I answer my phone to hear, "Her ex-fiancé, Logan Michaels." I disconnect as the doorbell rings again. "It's your ex," I say. "Get dressed." I slide my phone into my pocket and snatch up my shirt, tugging it over my head. "I'm not in the habit of getting a woman ready for another man."

When I would move away, she grabs my arm. "Really? Did you really just say that to me?"

"What do you want me to say?"

"I want you to not be an asshole. There's nothing between me and Logan. *Nothing*. And besides, fucking me to get through the trial doesn't exactly give you a say in what I do anyway."

And yet I seem to want one, I think but what I say is, "And yet he's here."

"I don't know why. I don't even take his calls. He wants something. He's my father's protégé. That's how they operate."

"Like I said—"

"Not me," she snaps. "He doesn't fight battles he can't win." Her cellphone starts to ring. "That's going to be him," she says. "When I don't answer, he'll leave."

We stare at each other, the air pulsing between us as the phone rings and then goes to voicemail. Aware that Logan could be tapped by Waters in some way or some game, I say, "Listen to the message."

"No, I—"

"We need to know what he wants."

Her lips press together, her eyes searching my face before she concludes, "You think Waters got to him."

"If you're out of his life—"

"I am."

"Then I don't like how it reads with him suddenly showing up. We need to know who's vulnerable to Waters' influence and who's not. Check the message."

She doesn't need further nudging and to my surprise, she plays the message on speakerphone.

"Pri, if you're home let me in. I need to talk to you. It's about your father. It's urgent."

"My parents are worried about the Waters' case," I say. "He's now tasked with scaring me straight, so to speak. Straight out of the DA's office."

Another time, I'd ask her why she left the firm, but right now, Logan is outside the door. "Be sure," I say. "Talk to him. I'll hide."

"I hate this," she murmurs, but she doesn't argue.

Logan rings the bell again and she scrambles to get dressed, almost done when her phone rings again. She glances at the caller ID. "It's him." She answers. "Why are you here, Logan?"

The phone is close and Logan is loud. I clearly hear his reply of, "Just open up, Pri."

Her name on his lips irrationally irritates me.

"Give me a minute, Logan," she says, disconnecting and setting her phone on the hall table before sticking her gun in the drawer.

Her gaze scans and lands near my feet, and fuck me, she squats right in front of me, her face at my belly. She's trying to kill me, I decide, a point she proves when she stands, grabs my hand, and shoves her panties into my palm. "I'm going to fall over if I try to put those on." She squeezes her eyes shut and then blinks up at me. "And my God, I just squatted in front of your crotch and handed you my panties, didn't I?"

My cock is officially ramrod hard again and I pocket the panties and step into her, my hand sliding under her hair and settling on her neck, my lips lowering to hers. "Better you give them to me than to him. And better my tongue than his." She gasps and I laugh, kissing her hard and fast before I thumb away the lipstick on her cheek and say, "Get rid of him quickly."

I don't wait for her reply, hurrying into the living room where I grab the champagne bottle by the neck and then finger the glasses with the opposite hand. The champagne goes in the fridge, the glasses on the island before I step into the hallway that runs behind the kitchen and the living room. I'm flat against the wall, just outside the foyer when Pri opens the door.

"What are you doing here, Logan?" she demands.

"Are you going to invite me in?" he asks.

She seems to hesitate. "For a minute," she says primly.

The door creaks and footsteps hit the foyer before the door shuts again. "Are you alone?" Logan asks.

"Yes, I'm alone," Pri replies testily. "Why?"

"Because you have that freshly fucked look that always made me want to fuck you all over again."

My fingers curl by my side, and I decide right then that Logan Michaels will never touch Pri again, not as long as I'm alive.

WHEN HE'S DIRTY

Chapter Sixteen

PRI

My anger at Logan comes at me hard and fast, the history of our relationship an easily sharpened blade that cuts right to my core.

"Careful, Logan," I warn, wanting to smack the blond pretty-boy right on his clean-shaven jaw. "I'll show you my knee and we both know I'm good at putting it in just the right place."

It's a reference to one of our final fights when I'd had enough of his controlling ways, which too often got overly physical.

His lips curve in amusement, the air of arrogance a second skin he wears right along with his expensive blue suit. "You are," he agrees. "You surprised me, but I suppose you had a right to be angry that night."

"You *suppose*?" I challenge.

"Looking back gets us nowhere, Pri. Looking forward, everywhere. How about you invite me to the living room for a drink?"

"No drink," I say, folding my arms in front of me, acutely aware of the draft up my skirt and the fact that I handed my panties to Adrian, who is still in the house. "You need something," I add. "What?"

"Come on, Pri," he coos in a low, seductive purr that used to work on me. It doesn't anymore.

Apparently, tall, dark, and deadly with a goatee and tattoos, is what works on me now, considering my body is still thrumming from Adrian's touch.

"Let's sit," Logan prods.

I clench my fist by my side with the realization that he's not going to leave until he says his piece. And the truth is that I need to know all I can about anyone or thing that equals vulnerability to Waters, including Logan. "You have five minutes," I say turning away from him, leaving the door for him to handle and walking to the living room.

I round the couch and sit in the chair Adrian had been sitting in, wishing I hadn't put my gun in the drawer before opening the door. Somehow, my gun on my person just feels better. Not that I think Logan wants to kill me, but it would keep him from getting handsy, and he likes to get handsy. I don't even know how Adrian would handle that. Would he just let it happen? Not that it matters. I don't need anyone to save me from Logan. I've already proven myself quite worthy of that task.

Logan joins me but doesn't give me space. He sits down on the coffee table in front of me, too close for comfort. "We need to talk about the Waters' case."

Beneath the surface, I bristle, but my courtroom face slides into place. "I'm not at liberty to discuss the Waters' case with you and you know it."

"I'm not asking you to discuss details. One of my clients came to me with a warning. He told me that you need to step away before it's too late. And no, he didn't elaborate but considering you have two dead witnesses and a clusterfuck over there at the DA's office, we can both use our imaginations."

My heart punches at my chest. "Which client?"

"It doesn't matter and I know you know I can't tell you that. I talked to your father. We want you to come back to the firm."

I laugh bitterly before I can stop myself. "And my father thinks sending you to convince me will work? But then he really has no idea how badly we parted ways, does he? To him, all you did was fuck my secretary."

He ignores my reference to our history and moves right past it. "He would've come himself but he says he made a pact of some sort with you."

It's not a false statement. After a year of turning every holiday or family get together into the hell I was avoiding, my father agreed to shelf the topic to save our relationship. On the surface, it worked.

"I went to bat for you," Logan says. "He wants you back. I told him to show you he understands what you want from your career and the firm. I believe, I really do, that if you tell him you want your own division, he'll give it to you. You pick the cases. You pick the staff. You have your own budget. I set the groundwork."

"Even if he would," I say, "even if I'd consider coming back, which is highly unlikely, I'm not walking away from this case."

"Hand it over to the DA, who's a pussy for having you frontline this. He's protecting himself, his career and his life, and making you the fall guy. I'm worried about you."

No, I think, studying his face, he's not worried about me, but he is worried. Whoever this client is that warned me off the Waters' case, Logan wants to please them. Or rather desperately needs to please them. Suddenly, it hits me. I know what this is about. The trade Waters offered me, the attorney linked to a long list of suspected money laundering schemes. "You're representing Jason Whitaker."

He leans back instantly, his spine stiffening. "My clients have nothing to do with this."

"That's a yes. My God, you never cease to surprise me. You can't do anything honestly. It always has to be sneaky." I stand. "Go home, Logan. Call me tomorrow at work and we'll discuss your client's potential dilemma. Maybe we can make a deal if he can give me something to use against Waters."

His eyes bore into me. "When did you become such a bitch?"

"I'm pretty sure it happened about the time you buried yourself in my secretary on top of my desk."

"Step away from the case," he bites out.

I read beneath the words and say, "Or what?"

"I can't promise to protect you."

"You never did. I protect myself. Go home, Logan."

He scowls and seems like he might argue, but finally turns on his heel and marches toward the door. I follow, and when he exits, I shut the door, locking it and leaning on the hard surface. Adrian is there almost instantly—tall, dark, and alluringly dangerous. His hands settle on the door on either side of me and I'm suddenly aware of how on display my past defending people like Waters is right now. "How much did you hear?"

"All of it," he says, but he doesn't comment further or ask a question. He just watches me with his dark brown eyes, unmoving, more stone than man, and I want to reach inside him and dig for his thoughts.

"What are you thinking, Adrian?" I whisper.

His hands come down on my neck, over my hair and he drags me to him. "What do you think I'm thinking,

113

Pri?" he asks, his breath a hot tease on my lips, a promise of a kiss that doesn't come.

My fingers curl in his T-shirt. "I don't think I want to know right now."

"No?" he challenges, stroking my hair from my face and tilting my gaze to his. "Well, here's a hint: none of it includes giving your panties back."

Heat flushes my skin, and I push to my toes. "Then kiss me already," I say, not ready to face the blade from my past that just keeps cutting.

But he doesn't. He doesn't kiss me. His mouth lingers above mine, the air pulsing around us, time ticking like an old man walking a mile up a hill, so incredibly slow. I'm confused. I'm uncomfortable. I'm desperate in ways I don't remember ever being desperate.

"Or don't," I say. "And just let me go."

WHEN HE'S DIRTY

Chapter Seventeen

ADRIAN

"You may wish I did," I say softly, "I may, too." And then I do as she's bid. I kiss her, licking into her mouth, and damn, she is like tasting heaven while I'm being pulled into hell. Because while she clearly believes she's sinned, she has no idea what that even means. She is good and I am not, but damn it, in that one stroke, I'm drowning in Pri, lost in her, molding her closer.

And she doesn't need to be won over. She's kissing the hell out of me, tugging at my shirt. I yank it over my head and toss it aside, reaching for her blouse. We're all over each other, ripping at clothes. Touching. Tasting. I scoop her backside, squeezing that sweet little ass of hers, and drinking her in, savoring her as I do.

My lips part from hers and for a moment we just breathe together, and I swear right then, I feel something with Pri I have not ever felt in my life. I don't even know what the hell she is doing to me. I know I should stop. I know she'll hate me later for a hundred reasons, but I can't seem to care right now. I shove the lace of her bra down and pinch her nipple, swallowing her gasp. I reach for my pocket and a condom. She's working my zipper and then her hand closes around my cock, and I'm long gone, past the point of no return.

My pants stay put. So does her shirt. Everything that can be shoved aside is shoved aside and my fingers slide into the wet, slick heat of her sex before my cock follows. And holy fuck, she feels good, hot and tight and soft in all the right places. I lift her and her arms come around my neck. I'm not doing this here, with her against the hard-ass wall. I carry her to the living room and lay her on the long lounge chair, going down with her, on top of her. And that's all the willpower I have. I thrust into her, my hand under her backside, squeezing and lifting, arching her into my pumps and grinds. She moans and bites and kisses. She's as wild as I am, present, accounted for, and so damn hot. But I'm present and accounted for as well. I'm aware that she's Priscilla Miller, with intelligent blue eyes, long brown hair, a runner who smells like flowers with a stubborn, tormented personality, and a love for a white mocha. And even now, fucking her, driving into her, somehow knowing these things only makes me want her more. I don't want that little bitch Logan to fuck her. I don't want anyone but me fucking her. And that's crazy, so fucking crazy, but still, I slow down and revel in that craziness. I slow us down. I slow me down.

I kiss a path down her jaw, to her neck, to her nipple—I lick it, suckle it, move to the other side, and repeat. She moans, her fingers diving in my hair, her back arching. Our bodies sway nice and easy now, and when she breathes out, "Adrian," I smile against her neck and whisper, "At least you didn't call me Rafael."

"Rafael never fit you."

I pull back and stare down at her, and it torments me, how well she once would have fit with me, the old me, the me before the Devils and I can't bring that me back. "No," I say.

"No?" she asks.

"No," I say and I don't know even know what I'm saying no to. I kiss her again and that slow and sexy thing we had going on is gone, replaced by urgency, and a pulse of something darker and harder. And so I pump harder, deeper, more furiously. And she is right there with me, arching into me, her leg at my hip, her fingers and nails digging into my back.

Too soon, and yet just in time, she gasps and then tenses. And then her body squeezes my cock, spasming around me, and I'm driving into her, my body quaking. She takes everything I am from me. I am completely lost and found right here, buried inside her. And then suddenly, it's over, and I catch myself on my forearms and bury my face in her neck.

I inhale her sweet scent and ease back to look at her, and I read the nervous energy in her face. She doesn't know what comes next. "If you meet my brother, call him Adrian."

"No," she says, a smile on her swollen lips. "He's no Adrian."

"You don't know him. Maybe he'll seem like an Adrian."

"I know that there's no one quite like you and that's a good thing."

"Considering I'm still inside you, sweetheart, that's good to hear." I roll us to our sides, pulling out in the process. "How about that champagne?"

"I do believe I could use a drink. We should talk, Adrian."

"You think?"

"Yes. I do. I'm not sure what we're doing but I'm certain it's complicated."

"You are correct. Which is why we should drink that champagne, order pizza, and then fuck again."

WHEN HE'S DIRTY

Chapter Eighteen

PRI

I've barely had time to pull my blouse over my head when my cellphone buzzes on the hall table. I grab it and glance at a message from Logan, something about lunch tomorrow. I ignore him as Adrian walks out of my hall bathroom, shirtless, inked, and beautiful, and then disappears inside the kitchen. I dash down the hallway to the bathroom, use it, and while washing up, glance in the mirror to find my lipstick all over my face. Good Lord, did it look like this when Logan was here? I decide I don't care. I don't want to go down the rabbit hole that is Logan's visit or the lines I've crossed with Adrian. Not right now. My sins with Adrian can't be fretted over and my father taught me not to fret over spilled milk. As he says, do the clean-up and charge forward.

I exit the bathroom and find Adrian still in the kitchen, filling two champagne glasses. "I grabbed the pizza magnet from your fridge," he tells me, offering me a glass that I accept, but not without my gaze sliding over his inked arms. God, he has a devil on his arm, not an ugly devil, but a devil or monster of some sort that is somehow beautiful. "I ordered two of your regulars," he adds.

I tear my gaze from his arm and meet his keen stare. "I eat pineapple on my pizza," I say.

"I heard. Works for me."

"It does?"

"I'm sick and tired of the same pepperoni pizza the guys' order. And yes, it's a devil, if that's what you're trying to figure out. I was that deep undercover."

"And you haven't gotten rid of it?"

"It reminds me of things I don't want to forget," he says, and when I want to understand, it's too late. He moves on, pulling out a stool for me and patting it. "Get cozy before you start drilling me for information."

"I'm not going to drill you."

"Yes, you are, but I'm tough." He pats his jaw. "I can take it."

He's all but inviting my questions, but somehow, I don't believe he's ready to give those answers. "Let's go to the living room," I say. "It's more comfortable."

"Sure," he says. "I have the bottle. You grab the glasses."

Once we're settled side by side on the couch, he motions to my glass. "Try the champagne. It's supposed to be sweet rather than dry."

I sip it, bubbles teasing my nose, sweetness touching my tongue. "It is. It's good."

He tries it himself and says, "It's not as stout as tequila, but it'll do." He angles my direction. "Joke time."

I smile, certain his jokes are distractions, ways to ease tension, and perhaps a segue to a deeper conversation. "I'm all ears."

"Do you know why Spiderman doesn't make a good boyfriend?"

"Why?"

"He's too clingy."

I'm not sure what the hidden meaning is to this joke, but I sense there is one. In fact, I bristle with the idea that he's warning me not to be clingy. "Are you telling me you're not boyfriend material? Because if that's—"

"I'm telling you that I'm not Spiderman. I'm more Batman who will beat your ex's ass if he acts again like he did tonight, and I won't be sorry when he cries like a little bitch. I'm also the guy who let the ever-so-moral Superman convince him not to kill Waters when I had the chance. And so, here we are."

I set aside his promise to kick Logan's ass and focus on what feels important. "Who's Superman?"

"My father. He was an agent."

I read the past tense. "How long has your father been gone?"

"Four years. He and my mother were killed in what was called a random mugging the year after I joined the Feds. I believe it was a hit."

"My God. Do have any idea who?"

He gives a negligible nod. "He had a good number of enemies. I tried to pin it down. I failed."

"Was your mother FBI as well?"

"She owned a bakery." He smiles a sad smile. "The biggest supplier of donuts to law enforcement that ever lived. And she was proud of my father." I can feel the shift in topic even before I understand it as he adds, "He believed that the law was best served by the book and within the system. We had to work inside that system."

A system my father taught me to manipulate, which is why I don't comment but rather ask his opinion. "And what do you think?"

"Waters is using that system against us and I knew he would. I can't turn back time and change what I did or didn't do, but now you're Superwoman. You have to get Waters because I let him go."

"The arrests and convictions from that sting are in the dozens, Adrian. Had you killed him, that may never have happened."

"Maybe," he says, cutting his stare for a heavy moment before he cuts me another look. "Maybe not. All that matters right now is that we keep everyone alive and we win the trial."

"And Walker keeps everyone alive."

"They're the best of the best."

He speaks of them as if it's them and him, but that's not how Blake spoke, that's not how Adrian's actions speak. "And you're one of them," I say. "You realize that, right?"

The doorbell rings and his hands settle on his powerful thighs. "That will be the pizza," he says, the moment to discuss him and Walker, and why he separates himself from them, lost. "You'll have to get the door," he adds. "I need to stay off the radar until the right time."

He stands and pulls me to my feet, and suddenly we are close, so very close, and we're staring at each other, a tug between us. There is something happening between me and this man, something I've never experienced. "I'll stay close," he vows softly.

I believe him, only I don't think he'll stay close for long. We both have a past, a dark stain, and I believe that we are kindred souls, bound together by those stains and a mutual enemy. But we are different as well. I'm the tree that weathers the storm and grows more roots, plants myself, and stays. Adrian can be likened to a majestic bird with a damaged wing. He'll fight through the pain, and then his wings will spread, and he'll fly away. And me and my roots will still be here, fighting the next battle alone.

I need to remember that.

Chapter Nineteen

PRI

The doorbell rings again and Adrian and I are still standing in front of the couch, staring at each other. We jolt out of the moment, and he presses cash into my palm. "That should cover a healthy tip as well."

I nod and cut my stare, hurrying toward the front door, in reality fleeing toward the front door with good reason: I'm afraid he'll read my reaction to our intimacy before I have time to understand it. The break is much needed and effective. My feelings are set aside for now, and a few minutes later, we're back in the living room, stuffing our faces while Adrian tells me ex-boyfriend jokes and I can't quite get back to the topic of him and Walker. We're on something like joke number six when I finish off my second slice of Canadian bacon and pineapple pizza.

"Do you know why ex-boyfriends are like Mondays?" he asks.

I groan with the expected punchline even before he grins and says, "They come too fast."

I decide right then that it takes a confident man to tell that joke, but then, he has reason to be. He knows how to handle himself naked—or semi-naked, in our case. I sip my champagne and watch him finish off most of a pizza and decide that while I might hesitate to tread on difficult topics, I need to know my star witness. "What's it like having an international superstar as a brother?"

"I'm proud as fuck, but he hit big when I was undercover and then after that I've been off the radar, waiting on the trial. I haven't gotten to celebrate with him."

"How does he feel about that?"

"Worried, but I promised him I'd be in the front row of his next concert once the trial ends. He has a couple of big holiday shows coming up, including one on New Year's Eve in New York. Maybe you can come with me."

"Maybe," I say cautiously, reminding myself that we're riding the high of a shared enemy. I'm not sure how that translates to real life. I'm not sure what this is between us. I'm not even sure it's a real invitation.

He cast me a curious, almost challenging look. "Maybe?" he queries.

"Maybe," I say. "If we're not bloodied and beat up by then."

His inspection is keen and his perception quick. "I get it," he says. "Ask me later." He changes the topic. "You're an only child?"

"You ask that like you don't know," I chide. "You've studied me, which is a little unnerving."

"You understand why," he concludes. "I know you do. Paper would only tell me so much."

"I know," I say. "I have two dead witnesses and innumerable horror stories about Waters to support your caution."

I don't offer more. I cut my stare and sip my champagne, not particularly eager to find out what I might read if I'm looking at him. My past work is a contradiction to my present, a contradiction to his role in law enforcement. I got bad guys off. Now we both put them in jail.

"What's the story with you and your father's company?" he asks.

And there it is: the Pandora's box of my past. "What you might expect," I say, glancing over at him. "I felt dirty. I needed out."

"What about Logan?" he asks, shutting the pizza box. "Is he the reason you felt dirty?"

"He didn't help," I say, deciding to just be honest. I need honesty in my life. "But no. I'd followed my father's career path. I needed my own."

"Fair enough," he says, "but back to Logan. Unless you'd rather not."

"He's suddenly in the middle of this Waters case, so I suppose he's a hard topic to avoid. You heard most of the story but I'll elaborate. He's my father's protégé. We made an obvious pairing. He proposed, and we were planning our wedding. I walked in on him and my secretary on my desk. He told me boys would be boys. I gave his ring back and told my father, who said boys will be boys."

"That's not true," he says. "You know that, right? I have buddies at Walker happily married and they are loyal to the bone."

"I don't know what I know about relationships at all anymore, other than I've done fine on my own."

He studies me several beasts before he asks, "How did you get to the DA's office?"

"A month after the 'boys will be boys' incident, one of the men I got off on murder, a guy I'd actually thought was innocent in this case, killed his wife. I was done. I quit and moved over to the DA's office. Two years later, I'm on what feels like the biggest case of the century."

"First," he says. "I've misjudged a few people myself and it's tough, but you aren't responsible for their actions."

"We both know that it's not that simple."

"No," he concludes. "It's not, but you're here now and the DA must trust you to have you lead this case."

"I saw inside the criminal mind at my father's firm. It's something I saw as a flaw, but Ed helped me see clearly. It's an asset against someone like Waters." This is my opening, my moment to face the elephant in the room head-on. I turn to face him, my leg on the couch between us. He sets his glass down and turns to me, his hand settling on my leg. I feel that touch zip through me, heat blossoming oh so easily. My gaze sweeps over the ink on his right arm, a similar gray, black, and red design with red flowers and a monster. This one features a skull. His fingers flex on my leg. "What do you want to know, Pri?" His voice is a gentle prod.

My gaze lifts to his, a spike of awareness in our connection. *About you*, I think. I want to know so much about him, and not as a prosecutor, as a woman, but I can't ask him for what he's not ready to give. "It's not what I want to know," I say. "It's what I need to say. I got some bad people off, Adrian. I don't want you to think that Waters can get to me. I'm a better prosecutor now for having seen the other side."

He studies me for several seconds and then his hand is gone and he's turned away from me, facing forward. I recoil with his reaction and I know what I have to do. "We need you to take down Waters. He can't be set free. I'll ask the DA to step up and take over the case. I'll step away."

"You aren't the problem, Pri." He scrubs fingers through his hair and then looks at me. "You are *not* the problem," he repeats. "I asked for that immunity agreement for a reason. I crossed the lines. I did shit. I believed I had to do everything I did at the time, but now, now I question it all."

I scoot closer to him, my hand on his arm, a silent plea that he look at me, that he open up to me. It's a big request, I know, when I of all people understand that love is often given more liberally than trust.

Chapter Twenty

ADRIAN

Pri's touch is like fire licking at my body and when my eyes meet hers, the rush of adrenaline and lust is as real and raw as it gets. But I resist her, wondering just how dirty she'll feel when she finds out just how dirty I had to get to take down Waters. Somehow it feels unfair to touch her again until she knows. I'm seconds from saying fuck it and kissing her again when she says, "You were undercover, Adrian."

The words are an unwelcome jolt of reality, her offering me understanding that is really an excuse, the same excuse I gave myself for far too long. I sit back, pulling away from her touch. I expect her to recoil. Instead—fuck me—she climbs on top of me, straddling me, trying to kill me as she presses the sweet vee of her body along the line of my crotch. My cock is instantly stiff and there's no way she doesn't know, but somehow, someway, I think of her, not me. My fingers curl at my sides and I don't touch her.

"What are you doing, Pri?"

She leans forward and presses her hands to my shoulders, pinning me in a stare. "Making you see me, really see me. And hear me. I need you to hear me. I defended monsters and I did it well. Nothing you tell me will make me hate you. If we're ranking good and bad, I'm just as damaged."

That does it. I snap, angry with her, angry with myself. I slide my arm around her, my hand finding her shoulder blades and I mold all those sweet curves into me. "You felt dirty. I *am* dirty. I'm bad. You're good. I shouldn't be here with you. Do you understand me?"

"Then why are you here?" she challenges.

"Because you're a damn witch," I say. "You just keep driving me fucking wild." I pull her mouth to mine, my tongue pressing past her teeth and she tastes like sweet champagne and innocence. She tastes fucking delicious. She moans and my cock twitches, her soft hands sliding up and down my arms. Oh yeah, she's a witch all right, a good witch being bad, and I want to fuck the bad right out of her.

But I can't.

I catch her arms and pull her back. "I don't have another condom. I didn't come to Texas planning to need it."

"I'm on the pill," she murmurs, "and I don't need your medical record, either. For all I know, Waters might kill me, too. For once, I'm going to live in the moment."

Logan's comment about her "just fucked" look or whatever that shit was he said grinds through my mind. A nerve tics in my jaw, an unfamiliar brand of possessiveness taking hold and control of me. I cup her face, tilling her gaze to mine. "Were you on the pill for Logan?"

"No. I do what I do for me, and I—I haven't—never mind. This is a bad idea." She starts to move.

I capture her waist and hold her steady. "You haven't what?"

"Had sex in two years, if you must know, I stayed on the pills because, well, I just did." Her hands come down on my arms. "Let me go."

The unexpected response has my attention. Everything about Pri has my attention. "Since Logan?"

"Yes. And don't start reading into that. I needed time for me and I took it."

Time to herself means time to heal. I know then just how deeply he hurt her and I have this ridiculous moment of jealousy, followed by a deep need to find him and punch him. Her hand presses to my face and I'm back in the moment, and I land there with one realization. She's recoiled all right, from men in general. Until tonight.

"And here I am," I say softly.

"Because I thought you were Rafael," she teases, but I'm not laughing.

This gorgeous, intelligent woman who is ten shades of damaged and sheltered in place to protect herself has offered herself to me, at least for "the moment" as she called it. She deserves better than me and she doesn't even know it. Proven by the fact that I'm too damn selfish to save her from herself and me.

My hands slide to her face and I dare to tell her exactly why I'm still here, and why I don't care about the way we complicate this trial. "I haven't chosen anything in my life in years," I say. "But I chose you, too, Pri." I kiss her then, and when my tongue slides against hers I can feel her soften against me, melting into a place we both crave—a place where tomorrow doesn't matter.

Our shared confessions seduce, provocative in their very nature and so is the way we undress each other. She's back on top of me, my hand low on her back, when I press inside her, I can taste her soft gasp on my lips. She slides down my cock and now I'm the one groaning with the tight, wet squeeze of her body.

"Damn, you feel good, Pri," I whisper, cupping her face, my lips at her ear. "Impossibly good," I add, my voice rough, my body pulsing inside her.

I mold her close, my hand low on her spine, my touch possessive, a brand I want her to remember. The air thicken around us, the connection I feel with this woman a living, breathing thing I cannot control. It's controlling me. I think it's controlling us both and inside the passion lives our pain. Two people, two kinds of pain, that are somehow lost in the passion. At least for now, we are the sum of a new beginning, two people lost in each other and it's powerful.

We lean into each other, our mouths colliding, tongues licking a seductive dance, an emotionally charged kiss that is nothing I expect and somehow everything I need. Hunger curls inside me and I thrust into her, pulling her hard against me. She gasps, and her finger flex on my shoulders. Desperation roars between us, humming in our bodies that grind together fast and hard, and then sway slow and easy. It's in those seductive moments that I feel Pri in a way I didn't know I could feel a woman. She feels it, too, and her body responds. She arches into me, burying her face in my neck, and then her body spasms around my shaft. I moan and thrust into her one final time, holding her as I shudder through my release.

When we're both relaxed, I hold her a moment, trying to figure out what in the hell just happened. What is this woman doing to me? I don't know my answer. And right now, I'm not going to try to figure it out. I roll her to her side, clean us up, and I'm aware that this is when I'd normally leave but I don't. I'm just not ready. I lie down on the couch, and take her with me, folding her close. Her head rests on my shoulder and her fingers tease the dark hair on my chest.

My lashes lower and I don't overthink this. I just hold her. That is until she whispers, without looking at me, "I defended the wrong people, bad people. So I really am bad, too." She hesitates and adds, "And I don't like that about me."

She's not bad, not even close, but this new confession, spoken thoughtfully and honestly, in an unsolicited and vulnerable moment, tells me just how deep her demons run, just how much guilt she feels. And no one can relate more than I relate, so I say the only thing I can say. "I understand the feeling, sweetheart."

She doesn't reply and I say no more, either. I mean, no one wipes away our pain by telling us it isn't real. Instead, I lay there and listen to her breathing grow steady and slow. She fades into sleep, and by doing so right after that confession, she tells me another truth. I was right. She trusts me. And I decide right then that I can't change what I've done in the past, but beyond that, I will deserve her trust.

And yet, the demons in my own past promise me that won't be good enough.

Chapter Twenty-One

ADRIAN

I fall asleep on my back with Pri naked and snuggled to my side, and wake to my pre-set alarm on my phone, the dim light of the lamp on the table above my head. Pri, all warm and sweet, is still pressed close, sound asleep. I shift us and grab my phone, turning off the alarm, and still, she sleeps, which tells me two things: her fear over Waters has affected her sleep and with me here, she feels safe. That's trust, which blows me away considering hours ago she was holding a gun on me and asking me if I planned to kill her mid-orgasm. I shift slightly and manage to stand, while she snuggles deeper into the couch, facing the cushions, the blanket I pulled over us hours ago, all that covers her naked body when I'd prefer it be me.

There is no logical answer for that and I force myself to turn away from her and hunt down my clothes. When I'm fully dressed, I return to Pri's side, and her breathing is deep, her sleep complete. I stand over her and stare down at her, long dark hair draped over the couch pillow, her skin pale and perfect. I know in my logical mind that I've seen many a beautiful woman, and fucked my share for that matter, but none of them affected me like Pri, none made me linger and hesitate to leave. None of them made me want to get to know them.

I glance at my watch, time ticking by far too quickly, and what I want doesn't matter right now. Watchful eyes do, and they see more during daylight hours. Pressed now, I consider leaving Pri a note, but that doesn't sit well with me and I don't believe it will with her either. I can't just leave. I sit down on the edge of the couch, my hand settling on her shoulder as I lean in near her ear, and damn, she still smells all floral and wonderful.

"Pri," I whisper.

She moans all soft and sweet and rolls to her back, blinking up at me, and says, "Adrian?"

Adrian, not Rafael. I don't know why her easy, groggy distinction means so much to me, but it does.

Her eyes roam over me and widen suddenly. "You're leaving?" Realization seems to hit her—disappointment I like a little too much, furrowing her brow. She scoots up to rest on the arm of the couch, oblivious to her naked breasts, as the blanket falls away, while I am not.

"Not because I want to," I say, pulling the blanket over her. "And not if you stay naked. It's just before sunrise and I need to get out of here under the cover of darkness."

She catches the blanket to her breasts. "We slept all night on the couch?"

"We did."

"You, too?"

"Yes. Me, too. I meant for us to talk strategy and plans last night but obviously, that didn't happen. I know that would have made you feel more in control and secure, but I promise you, we'll talk today."

She captures my hand. "You're not going to disappear, right?"

"Who's asking?" I find myself saying. "The woman or the prosecutor?"

"In all honesty? Both. Is that a problem?"

In all honesty.

Words I value.

Words I despise because I can never give her the same.

"No," I say. "That's not a problem. I'm not going to disappear. And now you know where to find me anyway. New York, working for Walker Security."

"Unless they send you to another country. We both know that's how you hid from Waters."

Obviously, she's been paying attention during our talks. "I'm here until this is over. For now, be you. Take your run. Go to work. We'll keep you safe. If you need me, call me or text me. If you feel even a little bit uneasy, or if you think you're in danger, call me."

"Are you sure it's safe for me to run?"

"We're here. You're safe. And the more normal you act, the better."

"In case someone is watching me?"

"I'm not going to sugarcoat this, Pri. It's Waters we're dealing with. You think you know how bad he is? You don't. Don't put anything past him."

"In that case, should I call you at all? Could the call be traced back to you?"

She's sharp. I like that, but she won't like my answer. "I'm protected," I say simply.

She draws a deep breath and exhales. "It's not your real number."

"I'm not going to disappear."

"That's a yes," she says tightly. "It's not your real number."

"Don't do that. I'm here. I'd stay here right now if it were possible. I'll see you soon."

"I guess I just have to trust you."

"And I have to trust you, Pri." I lean in and kiss her neck. "I trust very few people, but I choose to trust you."

With that, I force myself to stand up and walk away, heading to the back door, where I exit the house and reset her alarm. Any other time with any other woman, I'd say I didn't look back, but I do. I look back and the minute I'm in the Walker rental, I'm at the monitors where Savage is on duty, watching Pri's house.

"Any trouble?" I ask.

"All is quiet now. What happened with the dickwad of an ex?"

"He's representing the guy Waters wants to give up to catch a deal."

"And he thinks she's going to make a deal?"

"He thinks the DA might, is my take. He wants her off the case." Even as I make that statement, something is bothering me and I don't know what.

"I've got Blake on chat," Savage says. "I'll fill him and Lucifer in on the scoop." He glances up at me. "I'd make some crack about you getting to know Priscilla Miller in the deepest of ways, but I'm thinking you won't like that. She gets to you, aye?"

"This would be the time when I'd tell you you don't have the equipment to go deep, but you didn't go there, so I'm not going to." He chuckles and I start walking.

"Because she gets to you," Savage calls out. "And we can't save you. No one can. That's how this love shit works."

Love? What the fuck is he even talking about? I don't bother to turn around. I just call out, "I just met her Savage."

"That's what every lovesick pup says when he's denying he's capable of being a lovesick puppy. I know, man. I'm that puppy."

I wave him off and head down the hallway to my room, change into my running gear, and then end up in the small weight room that's set-up to work out before my jog. I've been at it for about fifteen minutes, and am presently curling a couple of dumbbells when Adam, ready for the day in jeans and a T-shirt, appears in the doorway. "Savage just gave me the rundown on Logan."

I set the weights down, my hands going to my hips. "Piece of shit tried to convince her to drop off the case to ensure Waters doesn't have the chance to hand his client over to the DA."

"Waters could still make the deal if she's off the case."

I draw in a shallow breath as a realization hits me. "Unless there is no real deal. Waters and Logan's client must be connected. This is one of Waters' plays. He just wants the case to get delayed until after the election. If Ed isn't re-elected, the new DA may not have the balls to pursue."

"That's where my head is at," Adam says. "And that's what I told Blake."

"And he said?"

"What better way to ensure Ed isn't re-elected but to kill him?"

"And what better way to ensure the next DA won't repeat the same mistake that got Ed killed," I follow. I pull my phone from my pocket. "I'll give Jacob a heads up." I punch in the text and my phone rings with Pri's number in my hand. "Pri," I say, glancing at Adam. "Make sure there's nothing on the security feed."

Adam nods and disappears and I answer the call. "See?" I ask. "I'm not going anywhere."

"That is good to know, but I wasn't testing you. I just wanted to say, I'm not going to run. I skip a day here or there. It shouldn't seem off."

"You're safe," I say, sitting on the weight bench when Adam re-appears in the doorway and offers me a thumbs-up on her safety.

"That's not it."

"Then why?" I press.

"Four reasons. Three of which are the champagne, pizza, and morning after sex effect. The fourth, I have work on my mind. I'm going to head to the coffee shop in about half an hour and get some work done. Something is bugging me about that entire Logan exchange. I need to figure out what."

My lips press together. I could tell her what's bugging her, and I will, but not on the phone and not when she's on her way out into the world, where she'll feel more exposed and vulnerable. Tonight. When we can talk it out. "I can't come. I've risked being out in public with you too much."

"I know," she says. "Besides, it's Rafael I have my coffee dates with. See you soon." She hangs up and I stand, glancing at Adam, who's holding the doorway up with his shoulder. "Coffee shop in half an hour. I need a fast shower." I close the space between me and him and he doesn't move.

"You can't go." He crosses his arms, stubbornly holding his position in the doorway. "You just told her that and you were right. As it is, you pushed your luck going to that party the night you met her. You could have been recognized."

"I knew who was there and I didn't stay long."

"You've been seen with her too often."

"Not by the wrong people," I argue, but I don't push. "I'll cover the outside. You go inside. I want you to stay close to her if I can't be."

"That," he says, "I'll agree to. You'll stay outside. Say it."

"I'll stay outside, asshole, now move." He backs away.

I pass him and call over my shoulder. "Unless you're getting your ass kicked."

Or, I add silently, since I seem to have staked an obvious claim on Pri, anyone comes at Pri the wrong way. For instance, her ex, Logan. That one I do believe I'd enjoy.

Chapter Twenty-Two

PRI

I choose a pink dress with a snug thick belt, fitted bodice, and flared skirt. I do so in an effort to appear to have a narrow waist, big breasts, and long legs. No. I do it to look good for Adrian. As my mother would say, I'm smitten. Ridiculously so. And I'm headed toward heartache if I'm not careful. But as I said last night, I'm practically on death row. I'm going to live while I can.

Once I've packed my trusty handgun and have my purse and briefcase over my shoulder, I secure the house and step outside, having already decided to walk to the coffee shop. I can't function in a bubble of fear, nor, as Adrian pointed out, does it send the intended message that all is normal with me. If I'm being watched by someone other than Adrian's people, they're at least still present. I'm safe.

The morning is nice, on the cooler side today, if that's what you call the seventies, though who knows if that will last. It's Texas. We celebrate when our legs don't burn on the car seat.

Once I'm at the coffee shop, I order a butterscotch latte with skim milk and settle into a chair at a corner table. Heavy on my mind is the deal Waters wants to make to hand over Whitaker in exchange for a lesser sentence, namely Logan's unexpected involvement. I don't have a history with Whitaker at my father's firm, and didn't know him to be a client, but it's a large firm. What I do have is a list of all the firm's clients at the time I left. I pull up my old computer folder, sipping my coffee while scanning the list and I find that I'm right. Whitaker was not a client. And why would he be? He's an attorney. He has his own firm. The whole situation feels off.

I decide that the places my mind is taking me right now lead to my father, and I don't want to believe that. In other words, I have to call him, which means I deserve a slice of chocolate bread first, which is a specialty here and quite wonderful. I push to my feet and slide my purse over my shoulder when normally I would not, but the gun inside feels rather special right now. Hurrying to the register while no one is in line, I place my order and move to the end of the counter. With my bag of warm, chocolate-iced bread in hand, I am on my way back to my table when a tall, burly man in jeans and a leather jacket steps in front of me. He's forty-something, with brown spiky hair, tattoos all over his body, and sharp, jagged features.

He's also familiar.

My lips part in shock with the realization that Joe "Rocketman" Mason, one of my ex-clients at my father's firm is right here, right now. The nickname is appropriate since he's no friend of the ATF, considering he runs an underground weapons operation I assume includes rockets, despite his denial, of course. I never liked him. I never willingly represented him, but my father forced my hand, which is another story altogether. Rocketman is not someone who'd be in this coffee shop at this time of the morning. He's more of a vodka and moves around during hell's nighttime hours kind of guy. "Joe," I say, my heart thundering in my chest. "How are you?"

"You tell me," he snaps.

"I—don't know," I say cautiously. "Am I supposed to know?"

"I hear Waters wants to start making deals."

I blanch, not shocked really since it's clear someone is leaking information, but unsettled. I also don't assume he knows this at all because what I do know is Rocketman. He's a bluffer. What concerns me at this point, is just how many people with criminal tendencies have skin in this game. "I can't talk about my case with you," I say, keeping my cool and giving him nothing

"You gonna make the deal?"

"I assume you have an opinion on me making the deal?"

"My opinion is my attorney should not be fighting Waters. Get off the case."

"I'm not your attorney," I say, and the timing of this, right after Logan's visit, is glaringly obvious since my father's firm still represents him. Obviously Rocketman has a connection to Waters, or maybe even Whitaker. "I am curious, though. What are you afraid of?" I decide to dig for his motivation. "Waters giving you up or you losing some sort of money train he somehow feeds?"

He gives me a deadpan look and then says again, "Get off the case."

"Just as I wouldn't desert you mid-case, which I didn't, I can't jump off this one. I have a duty now to the DA's office."

He shocks me by stepping closer, so close I can feel his hot breath on my face. Unsurprisingly, he smells like booze, though I can't say specifically vodka. "You won't be anybody's attorney if you stay on this case," he states.

Suddenly, Adam is there by my side, big and broad, his presence a crackle of power. "Introduce me to your friend, honey," he says as if we're dating.

Rocketman smirks and eyes me. "You really want your new man in on this?"

"She might not," Adam says, "but I do." Adam doesn't look at me, but he says, "Bathroom, Pri. Now." He nudges me to the left and claims the spot in front of Rocketman.

I don't wait around to find out what's happening. I take off for the bathroom, walking as calmly as my quick pace allows. Once I'm down the short hallway, I find the door in question, open it and rush into the large one-stall bathroom to find that I'm not alone. Adrian is waiting on me, shutting the door behind and locking it. He drags me to him, his hard body a welcome landing spot, one of his hands on my hip, the other on my face, his mouth closing down on mine, in a fast, hot, and wildly erotic yet somehow calming kiss. "Are you okay?" he asks, inching back to study me, real worry in his brown eyes. How did I think I needed to hold a gun on Adrian last night?

"Yes," I say. "I know him. He was my client at my father's firm. Embarrassingly, I represented an arms dealer. He goes by Rocketman. He wouldn't hurt me, at least not in public."

"An arms dealer," he repeats, his tone flat, his expression unreadable.

"Yes," I say tightly. "It was my job. The one I left for a reason."

"I know that," he says. "But because of that job, you should know that you never underestimate a criminal."

148

His hands come down on my shoulders. "You hear me? *Never.*"

"I know. I'm not naïve. I'm just saying he's smarter than to attack in public. And he's not a killer. He'd send someone else. He meant to intimidate me. He wants me to drop the Waters' case. Him here today, right after Logan was at my office, isn't a coincidence. I don't know exactly what's going on, but it's not what it seems."

Adrian rotates and leans on the sink, with me in front of him. "I think he's setting up a hit on Ed. If he dies before the election, the case may never be picked up by the next DA."

"It will," I say, "but it could take a very long time. There will be pressure to catch and convict the killer. There will be fear and chaos. The case against Waters will have to be rebuilt and it's flimsy now without me."

"If they even catch the killer. By having several criminals trying to get you to drop the case, it's harder to pin down who might have ordered the hit. I promise you, Waters has people around him who think they are doing him favors when he's setting them up."

"We're speculating here," I say, "and I'd discourage that, if we didn't have two dead witnesses and a series of questionable characters and behaviors involved."

There are three fast knocks on the door. "Adam," Adrian says, and he steps around me to let him in.

The next thing I know, I'm in the bathroom with two giant men and Adam's got my briefcase on his shoulder. "I got rid of Rocketman," he says, "but I didn't want to leave behind your work, considering the case you're handling." Before I can thank him, he adds. "I couldn't pin down his real agenda."

"He's a mouse on a wheel Waters is turning," Adrian says. "I'm betting that he thinks he's helping

Waters. Waters is setting him up to look like the hitman that takes out Ed."

"Are we really having a meeting in a bathroom?" I ask. "Should we go somewhere else?"

"We've had them in much worse bathrooms," Adrian assures me right about the time my cellphone rings.

I pull it from the side pocket of my purse and glance at the number. "Waters' attorney again. He apparently likes to call me early. I think I need to buy time for us to find Deleon."

"Agreed," Adrian says. "Time is good."

I nod and answer the call with, "No decision yet on the deal."

"Maybe we can make it more lucrative," Daniel offers. "Three for one."

"Who?" I ask, my eyes meeting Adrian's. "Who's he offering now?"

"Just offering a name gets around."

"Because you buzzed it around," I remind him. "I did not."

"I didn't buzz it around. See what I mean? Waters wants to talk to you. He'll decide if he can risk the names when he decides if he trusts you."

"Well, he shouldn't trust me," I say. "I'm not his friend."

"But he hears you're a woman of your word. Meet him. Maybe I can get him to give you someone even bigger."

I hesitate, the idea of sitting down with Waters not sitting well, but then I remember that clawing feeling I had for weeks before I caught Logan with my secretary. I knew something was wrong and it ate me alive. Once I knew the truth, it hurt, but I recovered. I faced the problem and stood taller. I have to do the same now. "When?"

"Three o'clock."

"I'll be there."

"Waters will be pleased," he says, and with that, he disconnects.

I glance between Adrian and Adam. "It's official. I'm going to meet the King Devil himself."

Adrian catches my hand and pulls me to him, his energy taut, his expression hard. "No," he says. "You're not."

"I have to do this."

"I will tie you up and hide you away before I let you sit at a table across from that man. Do you understand me?"

I could be angry. I could push back at how alpha and controlling he's being, but I don't. I know that he's lived in hell with Waters, and right now, I see those demons in his eyes, I see the torment they lay upon him every single day. And I can feel his genuine concern for me, perhaps as a man who lives his life as a protector, but I think also as a man. I press my hand to his face.

"Adrian," I whisper. "This is just a prelude to me facing him in court. It's good practice. People died because of this man. More will if we don't stop him and we need to buy time to catch his hitman. I have to do this. You know I do."

Seconds tick by and I watch those demons play in his eyes before he lowers his lashes, and I know in that moment that he knows I'm right. I have to face Waters, and the truth is, he won't be the first monster I've ever known, but that's not a detail I'd like to share right now.

Chapter Twenty-Three

ADRIAN

I know Pri feels like she's faced evil before, but Waters is evil incarnate, a man who sees an angel like Pri and wants a taste. I sure as fuck did. And yet, I know I really would have to tie her up to stop her from going and it's not like I could keep her like that without stalling the trial. Point for Waters. It's almost as if he knows I'm with her and into her. I hope like fuck that isn't the case.

"Adam goes with you," I say. "Non-negotiable."

"If I didn't know where this was coming from, I'd say you're being overbearing," she accuses. "You know that, right?"

"Damn straight, sweetheart," I say tightly. "On all other things we can battle it out and you may even win. Judging from how things have gone between us, you *will* win, but not when it comes to your safety. Not this. I'm keeping you alive."

"All right," she says, but she does so with a firm step backward, before she places me and Adam in profile, her arms folded. "Do we care if Waters knows Walker is involved?"

"We need to stay in the shadows for now," I say. "Adam's a master at becoming someone he isn't and dresses up real pretty. Can he go in as an ADA doing grunt work on the case?"

"He can," she says. "That works." She eyes Adam. "Does that work for you?"

"If it'll keep Adrian from tying you up before this is over, I'm all in."

Her cheeks flush. "I don't think he meant that literally."

Adam's lips quirk. "Of course not. I'll let you two talk." He winks at her, the dirty bastard, and then, dirty or not, a man of his word, he makes quick work of leaving.

The minute the door shuts, I lock it again and turn to face Pri, her pink painted lips begging to be kissed, but right now, I'm thinking about Waters—her face-to-face with Waters, specifically. She's not nervous enough about this meeting. She's not ready and I'm to blame. I was with Waters for two years and already I'm in her bed and playing protector. If she underestimates him as she has me, she'll end up dead.

"You aren't taking Waters seriously," I say, closing the space between us, my hands catching her slender waist, which is cinched tight over a pink dress that hugs her curves.

Her hands go to my hands at her waist, as if she's almost ready to push me away, which works. She needs to read my agitation and read it well.

"I take him plenty seriously, Adrian," she says. "I'm doing this to save lives. What is your problem right now?"

I walk her backward until she hits the sink, my legs caging hers. "I didn't ask for immunity for nothing. Don't underestimate me."

"I'm not afraid of you."

"Because I fucked you? Do you think that protects you?"

"Okay, that's it. I want out of this bathroom."

"Not yet. I'm not done with you. Is that what you're going to say to Waters? I'm not afraid of you?"

"I told you. I'm not naïve."

"And yet, I spent the night at your house. How easily you trusted me."

"Because it's you."

"Me? You don't even know me let alone what I did to ask for immunity. I know I have a certain level of protection and I'm still asking for it, Pri."

"I have your references."

"Blake knows the man I let him know and I learned that from the master himself: Waters." My gaze sweeps the curve of her breasts and lifts. "You look like an angel in that dress, Pri. The kind a man goes to sleep thinking about. He devours angels. He obsesses over how to turn them or hurt them."

"I'm not an angel," she bites out.

"He's sneaky. He'll seem like Prince Charming and he could kiss you while he's working to destroy you."

"He sounds like my father."

"Not even close. Your father manipulated you because he wanted you to follow in his footsteps. Waters wants you to kneel for him. And even if you do, you're just a disposable soldier. He will slice your throat and laugh about it."

"I've read his file. You remember that, don't you?"

"His file doesn't tell you shit. Why do you think he wants me dead? I know what you don't know."

"Okay. Can you let me off the sink now?" She presses on my unyielding chest and I catch her hands. "No. I'm not done with you."

"We're done. *Completely.* I made a mistake. You made your point."

My fingers tangle in her hair and I drag her mouth to mine, my hand pressed between her shoulder blades, molding her close. "What point is that?"

"You're dirty. I'm just bad. There's a difference."

"And here I thought you liked it when I'm dirty." I brush my lips over hers and she trembles in my arms.

"What are you doing, Adrian? I don't want—"

"I do. I want."

"An angel you can destroy?" she challenges.

I pull back and cup her face, tilting her gaze to mine. "Never. I will never hurt you. You know that. I know you know that."

"And yet you don't trust me to know better with Waters?"

"I've watched too many people underestimate him, Pri. I'm just trying to protect you."

"By being an asshole? I've got enough of those in my life, Adrian. I don't need another."

"And I've had too many people die in my life. I don't want you to be next."

She studies me, searching my face. "He really affects you, doesn't he?"

"*You* really affect me. I don't want your trust in me to impact how you see him."

"Then next time, just say that."

There's a knock on the door. "We have a line out here," Adam calls out.

I lean in and kiss her and she really is the sweetest thing I've ever tasted. "Change this damn dress," I order. "Wear something black and baggy."

She laughs and there's another knock on the door. "Seriously," I add. "Be careful."

"I will." She runs her hand over my cheek and when she tries to step away, I catch her hand again. "I'm sorry."

She turns back to me and pushes to her toes, kissing me. "You're not the monster you think you are, Adrian. Monsters don't stop someone from walking out a door to apologize." With that, she grabs her briefcase and hurries to the door, exiting while Adam enters.

"They all think I'm next in line," he says, shutting the door. "How the fuck are we going to walk out of here together without the line of women waiting outside thinking we're knocking boots or some shit?"

"I'll go first," I say, amused by his distress. "I need to protect Pri."

"You mean you'll go first because the last one out gets to explain what we're doing in here. You owe me on this one."

I'm laughing as I exit to find four women waiting. I wiggle an eyebrow at them and say. "He'll be right out. He has to fix his make-up." There are a couple of gasps that would amuse me more another time. Right now, I'm thinking about Pri's declaration that I'm not a monster. She's wrong and the only way to take down Waters is for me to prove that to her.

Chapter Twenty-Four

PRI

After leaving the coffee shop, I Uber home and change clothes.

Not that Adrian got to me, but I still feel more comfortable in a black skirt and black jacket with a cream-colored shell. Basic outfit. Basic attorney. I'm just going to meet Waters as part of a job. I decide that's how I need to approach this meeting.

I'm in my kitchen, finishing a slice of cold pizza, just like my old college days, about to punch in my request for a car when Adrian calls. "Did you change?" he asks.

"Why would I change?"

"You changed, didn't you?" he teases.

"Because you made me paranoid about the dress," I defend.

"I liked the dress, Pri," he says, his voice a low, rich baritone that reminds me of his hands on my body, his mouth everywhere. "Too much for Waters to see you in it, but," he adds, before shifting to all business, "that's not why I'm calling. Savage just finished up a meeting with Ed to talk about the seriousness of the threat against him. Savage is going to be staying with him until this is over."

"I'm honestly shocked," I say, perching on a barstool. "I mean, I assumed he'd accept protection to some degree, but I thought it would be harder than that. Ed tends to play macho man and so far he's declined protection."

"Savage scared the shit out of him, which isn't hard for Savage. Deleon won't win if he comes at Ed when Savage is around."

"Is he openly protecting him?"

"No," he says. "We want to maintain a covert operation to surprise Deleon."

"I assume Ed doesn't know about the Waters meeting?"

"No. I didn't talk to Savage until after you left the coffee shop."

"I'm hoping that talk with Savage really did scare him, and therefore he'll be in the right state of mind to discuss the Waters meeting."

"You think he'll want to make a deal?"

"I think a three for one right before an election will sound appealing."

"Waters won't make a deal. Not unless it's something insane that gets him right back on the street and that would make the DA look stupid."

"I don't think Ed would make a deal that got Waters back on the street on his watch, but ten years from now, maybe. That's my fear. A sentence of twenty years with good behavior might allow that the happen."

"Waters won't agree to ten years. He'll kill Ed off first, which means I'll have to convince Ed not to be stupid before he's dead."

"I don't want to know what that means, do I?"

"It's better than dead. Feel comforted."

"And on that note, a very slight change of topic. If Waters has Deleon coming for Ed, then at least the witnesses should be safe, right?"

"They're safe because they're with us and not in the safe houses, but Deleon isn't likely to be working alone."

"In other words," I say, "you just burst that bubble."

"They're with us, sweetheart. They're safe."

It's not the first time he's called me sweetheart, but this time it does funny things to my belly. I'm confused by Adrian after that bathroom encounter and that's not a good thing when I seem to be falling hard for him. "And you're all about the truth?"

"I haven't lied to you, aide from the name thing, and I won't."

"In other words, when you say you're dirty, you're dirty?"

"I did things I'm not proud of, Pri. You know that."

"Are you going to tell me what those things were?" I dare.

"Only the things that help you put Waters away."

That's an honest answer and I read between the lines. He doesn't want to tell me anything but will for the greater good, and that really is where his head rests. He could easily push for a deal for Waters to save himself the hell of his confessions, but he's not. I mean yes, he'll be granted his immunity deal, but even with that in place, the world will know his sins. The burden is great. His bravery greater.

"I'm speaking to you personally right now, Adrian," I say, "not as a prosecutor, but as a woman. One day, when this is over if you ever want to talk about it, I'm here."

"I won't. You need to know I won't."

"And you need to know that I'm okay with that, too."

He's silent a moment and then he says, "You are not what I expected."

"You keep saying that."

"And you keep proving me right."

"And that's still a good thing?"

"It is. And so are you. I'll see you sooner than you expect."

I open my mouth to ask what that means, but he disconnects.

Chapter Twenty-Five

PRI

Once I'm at the office, I unload my bag at my desk and head to the breakroom for coffee. I've just finishing doctoring a steaming cup my way when I hear, "Anything I need to know, boss?"

At the sound of Cindy's voice, I turn to find her joining me, looking pretty and petite in a pink dress. I'm not sure what the universe is telling me with her choice of attire, but I'm pretty sure it's laughing at me.

"What you need to know," I reply, avoiding the topic of Waters, "is that coffee makes the world go round and," I sip from my cup before adding, "never put tequila in it before going to talk to the DA, even when tempted."

She lowers her voice conspiratorially. "Is there tequila in your coffee?"

"No," I laugh. "I wouldn't be standing."

"Oh true. I've seen you drink."

"Barely."

"Exactly the point. What's happening? Why are you meeting with Ed again?"

"I'm shocked you don't already know since the defense likes to spread gossip like it's butter on hot bread."

"Okay, you're killing me here." She shoves her hands to her hips. "What don't I know?"

"Waters wants to meet. He's offering up three for one."

"Holy wow. Who? Which three?"

"He won't say until he trusts me, which supposedly he can decide just by meeting me."

"He asked for you, not Ed?"

"He did," I say, and it hits me how interesting that is. Why wouldn't a power-hungry monster like Waters ask for Ed? "But it doesn't matter who he wants to talk to," I add. "We aren't making a deal."

"You sure Ed's going to agree with this? It's three for one."

"Yes," I say, though I'm not, but I'll fight him on a deal. If I don't, Adrian will and I'm not sure what that means or why it doesn't bother me.

"Yes? I mean, Pri, maybe this can work out. Get him and three other bad guys off the street for a decade or more. It could work."

"It won't work."

"Why?"

"Aside from ten years being nothing for a monster like Waters," I say, "there are things at play here you don't know."

"What things? I'm supposed to be learning. Teach me, please."

Any other time, I would, which is why she isn't going to stop pushing. It's not in her nature and I've invited her to use that nature. "I'll explain when I can."

"When you can?" she presses.

"Accept the answer, Cindy."

Now her lips press together. "Can I go with you to see Waters?"

"No. He's dangerous. He eats pretty little girls in pink dresses like mints."

"I'm tough and unafraid. You know this."

She's right, I do. And I also wonder if I sounded as cavalier and cute when I took the same stand. "No," I say. "People have died. I'm not risking you being a target as well."

"I think you're the real target. You the one he's asking for. You die, the case slams to a halt."

"Well, *thank you* for keeping it real."

"I'm simply suggesting multiple people at the meeting dilutes the focus."

"No," I say again and I set my cup down, deciding I've had enough caffeine. "I need to just get this done with Ed. Please go make sure the team is in full swing."

"Got it. I will. Good luck."

Luck, I think as I step into the hallway, won't save me, not from Waters, or the way I'm tumbling down a rabbit hole with Adrian, a man who openly tells me he's dirty. That's not the story Blake or Adam tell me, though. No wonder I'm confused with Adrian.

I turn the corner to Ed's office and pass the empty secretary's desk when two men in suits exit his office: Agent Pitt and Josh Martin, Grace's new man, the detective that just left the department and went into private security.

"Just the person we were about to come and visit," Agent Pitt says, he and Josh claiming the spot directly in front of me.

"Good to see you, Pri," Josh greets, offering me his hand, which I shake but I'm uneasy for no good reason. I know him, albeit not well as Grace does. The DA's office is large and our cases simply never collided.

"I thought you took another job?" I ask.

Pitt interjects. "I suggested Josh talk to Ed and the US Marshals department about adding a layer of private security protection for the witnesses. Ed says you have that handled."

And now I know why I'm uneasy. Ed ran his mouth, he trusted outside the circle that Adrian claims is safe. "I have someone I'm considering," I say quickly, trying to save this. "But truth be told," I add, "I'm not overly comfortable bringing someone else in who might be compromised."

"Ed indicated you've already made a hire," Josh says. "If that's not the case, I'd like to take you to lunch and talk it out."

"Not today," I say quickly. "I'm booked. Call me tomorrow and we can talk."

"What about dinner?" Josh presses. "Every moment counts when witnesses are on the line."

"She hired someone else," Pitt says, giving me a keen look. "Ed made that clear."

I purse my lips. "I need to talk to Ed," I say, glancing at Josh. "Call me tomorrow."

"I will," he says, and when I would walk into Ed's office, Pitt holds up a staying hand. "I need a word."

Josh lifts a finger. "I'll go say goodbye to Grace and be out of here. I'll call you, Pri."

I give a nod and he walks away as Pitt steps closer. "Who did you hire?"

"No one yet," I say. "I'll talk to Josh. Right now I have something pressing to handle." I take a step.

He catches my arm and when my eyes go wide, he immediately releases me. "Sorry. I'm sorry. I just—" he scrubs a hand through his hair. "Fuck." He shoves his jacket back and presses his hands to his hips. "I don't want this to go to shit. I know you don't have to include me in these decisions, but I'd appreciate it if you'd think about it."

His concern is palpable and as much as he frustrates me at times, I believe he cares and more than a little. So much so that if Adrian hadn't pressed me to leave him out of the circle, I'd feel compelled to pull him inside. Instead, I simply say, "I know this matters to you. I'll keep you posted the best I can."

"Which security company?"

"No one yet," I reply, hating the lie, but owning it for everyone's safety, but it may be too little too late. With that in mind, I push harder, lay down more of a show. "Anything from Adrian?"

"Nothing. I tried to call him and he didn't pick up. But before you freak out, I know he'll show up. He won't let Waters get away."

"Tell him I'll give him full immunity."

His brow furrows. "You think he needs immunity?"

"I've been thinking about what's holding him back. He was undercover for two years. He had to have crossed lines. Whatever I have to do to make him feel safe, I will. Even if that means hiring Josh or someone else. Just tell him I'll do what it takes."

"I'll reach out to him again."

"Thank you and please keep all of this under wraps. I don't need the possibility of us hiring outside security leaking to the press. It'll look like law enforcement can't be trusted."

"You think someone is leaking?"

"I think the walls have ears in a case this big. Please don't trust anyone. And I'm not even sure I'm a go on this idea of outside contractors."

"Why does Ed think you are?"

"He's a master of getting his way," I say. "Don't you know that?"

He studies me a moment, his expression unreadable, and then all he says is, "Talk to Josh."

He doesn't wait for a reply. He turns and walks away and as I turn to enter Ed's office I'm left with that uneasy feeling that won't let go.

ADRIAN

I'm sitting at the monitors with Lucifer, Adam, and Savage when Pri and I disconnect. Jacob, our man who arrived last night, is at the DA's office watching the building and Pri. "Something is bothering me," I say, setting my phone down.

"I vote Ed's the problem," Savage says, shoving the last bite of a stale donut in his mouth. "He vibed like a fish on cocaine."

"What does that even mean?" Adam asks before I can.

"So fucking jumpy he could have jumped right out of the pond," Savage says, kicking back in his chair.

"That's worse than my worst joke," I say. "And you just told him he's likely on a hitlist. Of course, he was jumpy."

"It wasn't that," Savage says, turning serious, his attention wholly on me now. "Something, as you said, feels off. What are we missing?"

I consider his question, when Lucifer says, "I think we need to look at everyone on Pri's team for this case. Anyone close to her that might be linked to Waters in some way. I'll get with Blake and see what electronic fingerprints we can find, but I need to know who she's the closest to. That feels like the highest risk."

"We need to do the same with Ed."

"I'm not buying the Ed theory," Adam says. "Why let two witness drop if he plans to help Waters walk?"

Which leads me to no place good. "Why is Waters asking for Pri and not Ed?" I ask.

"Isn't it standard procedure to have the lead ADA take these meetings?" Adam counters. "She's the defense attorney's contact."

"Waters is a power player," I say. "He goes for the top of the totem pole."

"Well then, let me state the obvious," Savage says, "Waters asked for Pri instead because he knows you're here, Adrian, and that you're doing naughty things with Pri."

Lucifer eyes me and says. "Gamble on the devil in the mix, man. Go with the worst-case scenario."

Adam simply gives me a small nod of agreement.

"Fuck," I whisper, and then glance around the room. "Lucifer's right. We have to assume the worst and that means Waters knows I'm here."

"So that means what, Captain Jack?" Savage asks.

"I'm not Jack Sparrow, Savage," I snap.

"Then where's the rum?" Savage says, but he's not looking at Lucifer. He's looking at me.

"About to be up your ass," Lucifer mumbles.

But I've been around Savage for two years. I know his word games. I get what he's saying when most of the rest of the world would not. "He means where's the payoff for Waters."

"And the answer is?" Adam says.

"I earned his trust and betrayed him. The rum, or rather his prize, is me. He wants to make me pay."

"And he's now focused on Pri," Adam supplies.

"It would appear that way," I agree. "And I'm suddenly glad I didn't kill him."

Savage frowns. "I don't follow. I find killing someone like Waters a good deed."

"He needs to be alive." I say, "for me to make him wish he were dead."

Chapter Twenty-Six

PRI

Ed is behind his desk and on the phone, his hair thick and scattered with just enough gray to be called distinguished. A man who wears a suit like he was born to wear it, a regular JFK type, good looking and powerful—three things that could work in his favor and aid his efforts to do good in this world. Too often life has taught me that those traits corrupt a man.

The minute his eyes find me, he scowls and ends the call. "Oh hell, what now?"

I shut the door and forget that he's my boss—or rather, right now, I just don't care. "Why are you running your mouth about extra security? I know Adam told you this stays between us."

He waves me off. "Pitt's FBI and close to this case and I've known Josh for his entire career."

"And if they justify the same of two other people you don't know and trust, and they're the wrong people, then what? Any chance Walker has to catch the assassin could be lost if Deleon gets a heads up. And then he might be so desperate he just comes after us."

"You're overreacting, Pri, which surprises me considering the number of extremely seedy criminals you helped stay out of jail."

I ignore the jab that changes nothing. "Call Adam and tell him what you did. Then tell me if I'm overreacting."

His jaw sets hard. "You're out of line."

"Out of line?" I demand, crossing to stand in front of his desk. "Do you want to die, Ed? Because I don't."

"Do you want off the case?"

"If that's a threat, we both know me stepping back from this case this late in the game hurts you and your campaign more than it hurts me."

"You're pushing me," he bites out, his energy crisp as an autumn day about to surprise you with a blizzard. "Is that really what you want to do?" he asks.

"What I want is for Waters to go to jail for the rest of his life, while we live ours. He's brutal. If he gets off, he still might come after us. Losing is not an option. Please call Adam, or I can, if you like."

"Call him," he says, passing the ball in what is clearly a power play.

I don't push back. I don't care who calls Adam. I just care that we call. I pull my phone from my pocket and dial Adam on speakerphone. "Pri," he greets and I can tell he's on speaker, likely with Adrian, as he asks, "Is everything okay?"

"I'm with Ed. He told Agent Pitt and Josh Martin, an ex-detective here with the DA's office, who is now in private security, that we hired private security."

He's silent a full three beats in which I can almost hear him cursing. "Did you tell him who, Ed?"

"No, I did not. Is this really a problem? Pitt and Martin are good men."

"Everyone's good until they prove otherwise," Adam says.

"Exactly what I said," he replies.

"Unfortunately," Adam says, "we often find out they're bad when someone ends up dead."

"Ed, this is Savage," comes another male voice. "Hey ya, Pri," he adds as if we've met, offering me power, I think.

"Hi Savage," I say, playing along and wishing I could speak freely and directly to Adrian, but comforted by his team's open involvement.

"The good news," Savage says, "is that our involvement means killing witnesses will feel too high-risk for the assassin."

"In other words," Ed says, a gloating smile on his face. "The assassin will back off."

It hits me then that this was Ed's. He thought Walker was wrong about keeping their involvement silent. And he thought exposing them was a way to protect himself, but I don't think Savage is confirming his success but rather the opposite.

"Speaking as a former assassin," Savage continues, "no. He won't back down. He'll decide he can only risk one last hit and he'd better make it good. That means you, Ed."

Ed visibly pales.

"But more good news," Savage adds. "I love these games and I always win. All the bad guys end up dead, Ed. *All* of them. I'll be close. Stop talking to people." The line goes dead.

Ed's jaw clenches and he stands up, no doubt flaunting his larger size. "Anything else?"

"Waters wants to meet. He's offering us a trade, three for one, him being the one. No names. He'll give them to me if he trusts me. And before you get excited about this, Walker believes anyone on that list is meant to be a suspect in your murder."

"Let me be clear, I agreed to protection because I'm not stupid, but it's borderline conspiracy theory that everything Waters does is a part of a bigger plot. Maybe he just wants to make a deal."

"You've read his file. This is what he does. He layers his many versions of evil. This fits his profile."

"I'll take the meeting."

"He asked for me. Waters said he'll only make the deal if he trusts me."

"I'm the final say. He can trust me."

"But can you trust him?" I press. "The deal will never happen."

"If it's a good enough deal, it might."

I blanch and recover quickly. "I can't even believe you're saying this. A good enough deal will put him right back on the streets."

"And put three other monsters behind bars. What time is the meeting?"

"Two."

"Good. We'll go together. Then he has you and me. We'll get this done and save some lives."

"You're afraid of him, aren't you?" I don't give him time to reply. "I'm not going. You're no better than my father. I don't even know why I'm here. You'd better make the deal because I'm off the case and without me, there will be delays. It won't look good that I quit right before the trial and your election."

"You think you can blackmail me?"

"This isn't blackmail, Ed. This is me telling you where I stand." I start for the door.

"Do not even think about walking out of this office," he calls out.

I pause, hand on the knob and I don't turn. "Are you going to let me run this case my way?"

"That's not how this works."

WHEN HE'S DIRTY

I open the door to exit and gasp. Adrian is standing there.

Chapter Twenty-Seven

ADRIAN

Pri pulls Ed's door shut behind her, her perfect pale skin flushed pink. "What are you doing here?" she whispers, catching my shirt and then glancing around me to check for prying eyes.

"Relax, sweetheart," I say, and do so with confidence. Aside from my team nearby and watching the building and even the floor, I tracked every person in my path and in view on my way here. "Ed's office area is private."

"And yet you walked through the main workspace. You're going to get yourself killed. Are you crazy?"

She's worried. I shouldn't enjoy that, but I really fucking do. "For you," I say, sliding my hand around her hip to press to her lower back.

"Adrian," she chides, her hands going to my arms, but her body softens and melts into mine. "What are you doing?"

"Weeks ago you would have eagerly handed me over to Ed as your star witness."

"I would have protected you then, too, but now—"
I arch a brow. "Now?"

"Now, I'm personally involved," she says quickly, glossing over what she might have said moments before. "We agreed you were keeping a low profile to *stay alive.*"

"And now, I'm not. Do you trust me?"

"I thought I did," she says, "and then you showed up here trying to get killed."

"More like trying to catch a killer."

"Please tell me you're not using yourself as bait."

"I'll tell you everything after we make sure Ed doesn't make a deal."

"That's a yes. Or no. No and no. You are not doing this."

"We can argue the merit of my actions over lunch after we leave. Right now, you just did your part to check the mistake Ed was about to make. Now it's time for me to do mine." I release her and when I would step around her, she catches my arm.

"Wait. Did you hear my conversation with Ed?" She gapes. "Did you *wire* the DA's office?"

"Savage did yesterday. He had a bad feeling about Ed."

"Oh. God. So do I. And?"

"And not much yet, but his sudden need to make a deal doesn't feel right."

"No, it doesn't. I tried to stop him."

"I know and that was pretty freaking badass, sweetheart. I'm just going to help you finish the job." I motion to the door. "Let's make that happen."

"How?"

"Trust me," I say.

She considers me a moment and then nods, and I can almost feel her concerns about Ed solidify with action. She turns, opens Ed's door, and enters.

"I hope this means you came to your senses," Ed spouts off to her, but I'm on her heels, right there behind her, shutting Ed's door.

His gaze rockets to me and he pops to his feet. "Who the fuck are you?"

"Adrian Mack, your star witness again Waters."

Ed's a good-looking guy who drips arrogance, and at some point, he had a backbone. But then Waters can scare the piss out of a rock. He glances between us, intelligent eyes reading the room before he narrows his stare on Pri. "You knew he was here and you didn't tell me?"

Pri doesn't even think about denial. She, as I expect of her, is right to the point. "He didn't trust you," she says. "Now, I'm not so sure that wasn't without reason."

By the time he turns his attention back to me, I'm in front of his desk. I lean over it, hands on the wooden surface, crowding him. He could back away, but he doesn't. He plays the tough, stubborn guy role and well. "What is this?" he demands.

"If you make a deal with Waters, he'll hunt me and anyone I love. And then I'll hunt you down and you'll be easier to find."

"Is that a *threat*?" he demands.

My lips quirk. "It's just me stating a fact."

Now, he leans back just a bit, obviously fighting the urge to put space between me and him. "Twenty years is not an easy deal."

"He won't take that," I say, straightening. "Obviously Savage wasn't clear on the cost to you, so I will be. Waters will kill you before he signs the deal and uses everyone he offered up to you as a suspect that offers him cover. After all, he's in jail."

"You don't know that," he argues. "You're jaded from your time with him."

"You're right. I am. But I know him. I know him well. Exactly why I'm your star witness. Are you willing to risk your life on me being wrong?"

His lip thin. "What do you want?"

"For him to go to trial."

"Bodies are dropping," he argues, his voice spiking. "I'm trying to stop the bloodshed."

"Including your own?" Pri challenges. "Because if you think this deal saves you, Adrian already told you it doesn't."

"And we can solve that problem anyway. We're going to catch the assassin. I'm going to go with Pri to see Waters. I'm going to tell him there will be no deal." I glance at Pri. "I'd leave you out of this, Pri, but you're already on Waters' radar and I don't trust Ed to face Waters and not wet himself."

"That's uncalled for," Ed growls.

"I'm not here to bolster your ego," I say. "I'm here to save your life, and most likely your career. You're going to back-up our claim of no deal."

"And if I don't?"

"I disappear again. And you don't want that to happen."

"I'm not feeling convinced of that," Ed snaps.

"Well then, let me change your mind. Without me, coming at you is his best chance of walking free. With me in the picture, it's not enough to end the trial and you. Another DA might or might not take the case. I will always step up to testify or to kill him, whichever comes first. If I'm here, he has to focus on me, not you. Convinced you need me yet?"

His jaw tics. "What keeps him from going after both of us?"

"He could," I say, "and will, but he'll focus on me first. Savage will remain your keeper until this is over." I lean back on the desk. "Let me be crystal clear. If I find out you made a dirty deal with Waters, I'll come for you. And I will make you pay."

"Are you threatening my life?"

"No," I say. "I think you being in jail and enjoying the benefit of so many new, close friends, would be a better punishment." I turn and motion Pri to the door, opening it for her before I turn back to Ed and say, "Waters told me a joke once, the only joke he ever told. How are an apple and a lawyer alike?"

"Are you serious?"

"How are an apple—"

"I have no idea," he snaps. "How?"

"They both look good hanging from a tree. I'd sit tight if I were you until Savage gets here." I pull the door shut and eye the text message on my Apple watch, grimacing as I do.

"What?" Pri asks urgently.

"Pitt left with Josh but came back. He just got off the elevator from the lobby. I don't want to run into him and have to answer a million questions. Go to your office and get your things. You won't be back today. There's a black SUV waiting on us downstairs. Meet me there." I start to turn and she grabs my arm.

"Be careful. *Please* be careful."

I step into her and cup her neck. "I have a reason to stay alive now. You. I'll see you in five minutes." I lean and kiss her hard and fast before I force myself to release her. "Five minutes," I promise again and then force myself to turn and walk away.

And I have no idea why it's so insanely hard to leave her. It is just for five minutes.

Chapter Twenty-Eight

PRI

I cannot believe Adrian's setting himself up as bait.

He matters to me. He really, really matters to me and I have this horrible feeling he's going to get hurt and I don't know what to do about it.

I'm all kinds of nervous as I enter the hallway outside of Ed's office area, but nevertheless, my pace is slow—steady, even—as I start my walk back to my office, intentionally pacing myself when I could easily run. I need to talk Adrian into anything but this insane plan of his that doesn't even make sense. What changed from this morning to now? It's still just morning.

Fortunately, I manage to find my way back to my office without interference, but as I'm packing up, Cindy pokes her head in the door. "Well? And who was that hottie that walked through the offices and disappeared into Ed's office area?"

The hottie must be Adrian because my God, he's gorgeous and confident, and the way he controlled Ed, who controls everyone else, was powerful. But I'm not talking about Adrian to Cindy so I say, "No deal," already thinking of ways to make my case for Adrian to go back into hiding, and my mind is on Waters' ex-girlfriend. "Any luck reaching Zara Moore?"

"None. She didn't just leave protective custody. She disappeared."

I set my purse on the desk. "Why do I feel like she's dead?"

"That's my fear, too," she says. "She tried to save herself by backing out of testifying and she never really had the chance. Speaking of which, Josh was just here. He and Pitt were trying to find out if you had already hired outside security for the witnesses. You didn't, right?"

"If I did it wouldn't be anyone connected to this office."

"In other words, you did."

I stand up and slide my purse to my shoulder. Grace pokes her head in the office. "Hey. Josh says he's been talking to you about some work?"

Cindy laughs. "He's working like he's on the catwalk, baby." She nudges Grace. "You two steaming up the sheets yet?"

My cellphone buzzes with a text and I glance down to read a message from Adrian: *Where are you?*

Trying, I reply back. *On my way.*

Meanwhile, Grace's cheeks heat. "I'm not talking about that."

"That's a yes," Cindy says. "And Pri already hired someone else."

Grace's gaze shoots to me. "You did?"

"I told Josh I'd talk to him," I say in complete avoidance mode. "And now, ladies, I need to go. I'm meeting with Waters and his attorney."

"With *Waters*?" Grace says, the blood draining from her face. "Do you have to?"

"I do," I say. "And it's good practice. I'll be in a courtroom with him for at least six weeks."

I'm now in front of the door, which the two of them are blocking, when Grace says, "I've been reading up on him. There are people who say he gets obsessed with certain people and won't let go. What if that's you?"

"I'm sure it will be. I'm the one sending him to jail."

"Are you really a prosecutor, Grace?" Cindy chides. "How do you operate when you're this afraid?"

"Alive," Grace primly replies. "You're too cavalier for your own good, Cindy."

"Ladies." I motion for them to move.

Cindy backs out of the doorway and I glance at Grace. "I'll be careful." I squeeze her arm. "Thanks for worrying."

She nods and hugs herself. I exit the office and start walking, while Cindy falls into step with me. "Sure I can't come?"

"Positive." I glance over at her. "And Grace handles white-collar criminals, has an IQ probably twenty percent higher than both of us, and a conviction rate higher than anyone in the department. You'd be smart to learn from her." I pause at the glass door leading to the reception area. "Go find Zara. Tell Pitt to find her."

She nods and I leave her there. I wave at Shari, our twenty-something super-efficient, feisty redheaded receptionist when a thought hits me. I halt at her desk. "Ed's assistant, Lynn. Is she in?"

"She's on a two-week leave."

"Vacation?"

"Yes. She won a cruise or something like that."

"Lucky her."

"Yes. I'm not that lucky. You gone for the day?"

"Most likely. Thanks, Shari."

About three minutes later, I step on the elevator, bothered by the cruise Lynn is on. I'm back to something just not feeling right, but I remind myself

Savage is now Ed's keeper. The elevator doors open to the lobby and to my displeasure, Logan is standing there. He, of course, looks like a Ken doll in a perfect blue suit, his jawline clean, his blond locks neat.

"I called you twice this morning," he snaps, accusation and demand in his tone, and I wonder how I once thought I loved this man. I'm certain I was mistaken.

He backs up to allow my path out of the car, which I accept. "It didn't hear it ring," I say, walking past him without stopping, toward the double glass doors and my final escape from this building.

Logan, of course, does just what Cindy did. He falls into step beside me. "I heard you're meeting with Waters today."

In other words, I think, Waters' people are running their mouths, but that doesn't surprise me. It supports the theory that Waters is setting up a suspect list before he has Ed killed. Still, I play along. "Who told you that?"

"I have sources," Logan says. "Step back from this before it's too late."

That statement's telling in that it shows no concern for his client he believes to be one of the trades Waters wants to make. We reach the glass doors, and thank God, someone holds the door for me and I'm outside before Logan. Unfortunately, he's fast and immediately in front of me, blocking my path. "Come back to the firm," he says. "I talked to your father again. He's all in on you running your own division."

"Clearly you have cards in this game. What is really in this for you, Logan?"

"Your safety." He lowers his voice. "I miss you. I'm worried about you." His hand comes down on my arm and I step back, out of his grip.

"No," I say. "And whatever deal you made with the King Devil, which it's obvious you did, you better hide now. He'll come for you when you let him down. And having Rocketman visit me was not cool Logan."

His expression registers surprise, but he's a master actor, and I am not fooled when he asks, "Rocketman visited you?"

"Don't play dumb. I know you know. He sounded just like you."

"I told you, there's buzz out there that you're in danger. And I didn't make a deal with Waters. A lot of bad people fear they're going down if Waters goes down."

"Your people, right?"

"That's not the point. You're in danger," he repeats.

"You mean you're in danger if you don't make me listen."

"We're connected. I go down. You go down. Your parents go down."

I don't want to be affected by his words, but I'm concerned for my parents. I'm also all too aware of the way Adrian is setting himself up as a target, refocusing the danger on him. It's brave. He's brave. And there are things going on here I need to talk to him about now.

I refocus on Logan. "I need to go." I step around him and start walking, my lips parting in surprise at what I find: Adrian, out in the open, leaning on the black SUV he'd promised awaited me. And my God, he's gorgeous. Dark and ravishing in jeans and a T-shirt, his inked arms, his goatee. He's dangerous, I know, but while he claims to be dirty, the only dirty I've known him to be, I liked.

"Who the fuck is that?" Logan demands as he figures out I'm walking right to Adrian.

Adrian pushes off the vehicle and steps into me, his hand possessively settling at my hip. "Ready?" he asks, his eyes warm, even gentle, when they meet mine, but his energy is sharp, almost threatening. He is not pleased about Logan.

"Who the fuck are you?" Logan demands.

Adrian's lips quirk and his eyes meet Logan's. "Your worst nightmare," Adrian replies, "if you do anything to hurt her. Any questions?"

Chapter Twenty-Nine

ADRIAN

There are men and there are boys in men's bodies. Logan's a boy in a man's body.

He stares me down, a fool who thinks he's a big fish, but what he doesn't understand is when a fish swims among the sharks long enough, eventually a shark catches him. I'll be that shark if he's not careful.

"I never hurt her," he claims, but he cuts his stare for the briefest of moments, a liar's tell. He not only hurt her—he knows he hurt her.

"We both know you did," I say.

"Who are you?" Logan demands again.

"No one you can call friend."

Pri tugs my arm, trying to garner my attention. "We need to go. *Now.*"

I don't look at her, my gaze remaining on Logan. "You heard the lady," I say, my lips twitching. "We need to go."

I turn away from him and help Pri into the backseat, while Logan calls out, "Pri, damn it. We need to talk. Think about your parents. Think about keeping them safe."

Attention-hungry bastard. Now he has mine. I turn back to him. "Play this game cautiously, Logan. It's a dangerous one." With that, I follow Pri into the vehicle, and pull the door shut.

Adam is behind the wheel and I motion him forward. We're already moving when I rotate to face Pri to find her angled in my direction, waiting on me. "What are you *thinking*?" she demands. "What was that? What are you doing?"

I scowl, bristling at her attack. "Are you protecting him?"

Her brows dip. "Who? Waters? I'm protecting Waters? What are you talking about?"

"What are *you* talking about?"

"You," she says. "Who else? I'm talking about you putting yourself out there for bait. Why? Why is that necessary? You don't get to come into my life and make me care about you and then just die." She pokes my chest. "You don't get to do it, Adrian."

She's talking about me, not Logan. She's protecting *me*. My temper burns out in about two seconds, and in that moment, I recognize how alone she's been since Logan burned her. And yet, she let me in.

"Did you go along with this, Adam?" she demands, tapping his seat from behind.

Adam eyes her in the rear-view mirror. "I plead the fifth."

"That's a yes," she says. "He's your friend."

I slide closer to her and catch her waist, my hand settling on her lower back, molding her close. "I'm going to be fine. And I'm not going anywhere. I'm here."

"Until this is over or you're dead. You made yourself bait."

"I'm not going anywhere," I repeat. "And I have resources and a team, friends like Adam to protect me. And you and your family. Blake had the foresight to send a few men from our Dallas office to Austin at dawn. They just got here and they're already in place."

"How many?"

"Four men, good men. We now have full-time attention on your parents in doubles, without them knowing. They're protected. You're protected. I'm protected."

"But Deleon—"

"Will come for me and not anyone else," I say. "I have a plan, but we need to talk through pieces of that puzzle. Overall, you'll feel better about all of this when you meet our team. Which is why," I add, "now that we have more men and coverage, and I'm out in the open, you can meet them. Unless you object, we're on our way to meet Jacob, Savage, and Lucifer for lunch."

Her eyes go wide. "In public?"

"Yes, Pri," I laugh. "In public." I motion to Adam. "Though Adam and I can tell you, taking Savage out in public is not always a good idea. You'll figure out why over lunch."

"He's not kidding," Adam calls out. "Savage is Godzilla smashing through every place he enters."

"And he's guarding Ed?"

My lips curve. "Seemed a good match."

"Really?" she says. "Is it?"

"Savage is a killer and a protector," I say. "You want to be his friend, not his enemy."

"Truth," Adam chimes in.

"You okay with lunch?" I ask.

"Aside from now being intimidated by the idea of Savage, yes, but surely you're being watched. And as much as I hate you making yourself bait, won't all your men scare off Deleon?"

"Not a chance," I say. "I know him. I'm setting him up. He'll bring in his team to fight my team. And his team has nothing on Walker Security. It also means all of his men will be here where we can end them once and for all."

"That sounds dangerous," she argues. "And you're the target."

And her, I think, more so because of me. It's not a topic I welcome, but if I want to deserve her trust, I have to talk to her—alone. For now, I say, "I'm not going to die, Pri, and neither are you, but you need to know that I may kill a few people before this is over. You're going to have to live with that."

She presses her hand to my face. "Just stay alive, then maybe you'll figure out that I'm not a fair-weather friend."

I capture her hand. "Friend?"

"We *are* friends," she says. "Isn't that a good thing?"

"Yes, Pri," I say, surprised at how much I mean those words and how much closer to her I feel, as those words pull us together. "It is a good thing." And then, with none of the relationship hesitation of years and women past, I lean in and press my cheek to hers and whisper, "But we are so much more and I'm not letting you go."

She leans back and meets my stare, shocking me when my law-abiding prosecutor says, "Then kill him before he kills you."

"I let Waters go," I say. "I won't make that mistake with Deleon."

Chapter Thirty

PRI

The restaurant where me, Adrian, and Adam are meeting more of the Walker team is only a few blocks of heavy traffic and stoplights away from the DA's office in the downtown warehouse district. Appropriately, the bar and grill is a two-story warehouse, with plenty of front door parking thanks to the early hour of just eleven in the morning.

Adam pulls us into a parking spot and kills the engine. Adrian kisses my hand before he exits the SUV and helps me out, but once we're outside, I don't miss the fact that he, quite deliberately it seems, isn't touching me. I'd read into that, but I'm not sure what. Am I a conflict of interest some on his team won't appreciate?

Whatever the case, we join Adam on the driver's side of the vehicle, and with Adrian and Adam by my side on the walk to the door, I'd feel pretty darn safe walking toward the entry if one of the two of them wasn't on a hitlist. Actually, I might be on that same list as well, so overall, we're just like three ducks lined up to be picked off.

We enter the building through heavy wooden doors, the swoosh of cool air conditioning washing over us, and I breathe a sigh of relief that we are free of any bullet holes. Adam steps forward and greets the hostess, and Adrian's hand slides to my back, and I decide I imagined his withdrawal outside. "Ready to meet the team?" he asks.

"Ready to run away to somewhere with fall leaves, cool temperatures, and hot cocoa."

"I know a spot," he promises. "I can make that happen. *Soon.*"

I warm with the promise that radiates from his words and reaches his brown eyes. "Not soon enough," I murmur, but already Adam is motioning us forward.

With Adam in the lead, we track a path through the heavy wooden tables and walls lined with booths, and then up a set of wooden stairs. I glance down at the room below as we travel up, and I'm not oblivious to the fact that this is a planned seating arrangement. From what I can tell, from the balcony area above, we can see anyone coming or going. Once we're on the upper landing, my suspicions seem confirmed, as there are about eight tables, but only one, the long one by the railing, is occupied, and with three big men.

Soon, we're joining them, and all three men are on their feet and I'm introduced to Savage, Lucifer, and Jacob. My first impression is that they could not be more unalike. Savage is a huge guy, about six five-ish and solid muscle with a scar down his face. Lucifer reads a bit like a blond, tatted-up rock god persona, and Jacob comes off as straight, clean-cut military. We sit, me and Adrian at the end of the table, with Savage at the opposite end, while Jacob and Lucifer are to my right. I note the fact that on the inner side of the table, I'm the only one who doesn't have a full bird's eye view of the lower level. Right now, though, I'm focused on Savage. "Who's watching Ed?"

"Dude named Dexter." He hitches back in his chair. "He reckons himself—I talk Texan because I am Texan—he reckons himself a killer." He smirks as if that's amusing, but not in a way the rest of us understand.

"Dexter, Lucifer, and Savage all in the house on this one," Lucifer chimes in. "What could go wrong?"

"Right," I say, a tightening in my chest. "What could go wrong?"

Adrian squeezes my leg. "Everything for the bad guys," he assures me.

"Got that right," Lucifer agrees.

The waitress appears at our table and Savage grabs the basket of bread and lifts it. "We're going to need about five more of these." He grins up at her. "There's a big-ass tip in it for you." She laughs and gives him flirty eyes that he doesn't seem to notice because he's now looking at me. "Really nice to meet the lady that tickles Adrian right under the chin in the right spot and gets him warm all over."

I groan and cover my face with my hand. Adrian grabs it and kisses it, his eyes brimming with mischief. "Told you he's crazy, but you do tickle me in all the right places."

My lips curve. "Really?"

"And apparently," Savage says, "you even put up with his bad jokes. Or has he kept those to himself? Because, man, Adrian, you have to be real with her. Put that bad joke baggage out there. Let it shine."

Lucifer snorts. "Adrian can't help himself. I'll bet you a hundred bucks she's heard his jokes."

"You win," Adam says. "He hasn't kept them to himself."

Jacob smirks slightly and butters his bread. He's the quiet type, I decide, but in this crowd, someone has to be.

"All right then," Adrian says. "You all asked for it." He pretends to roll up his non-existent sleeves. "Since we have a prosecutor in the house, a joke for her. Did you hear about the two thieves who stole a calendar?"

I laugh. "No, I did not. What happened?"

"They each got six months," he says.

Jacob sets his bread down. "You get worse every day, man."

I laugh yet again and ease into the table banter that follows, ordering, and enjoying a delicious bowl of macaroni and cheese while Adrian and the rest of the guys all eat burgers. Savage's is disgustingly rare and my disgust amuses him. It's a good lunch, and if Adrian wanted me to feel support, I do feel that and more. I feel like I'm a part of a team that's come together to take down Waters once and for all.

When the plates are clear, Adrian focuses on me, and so does the table. "Let's talk about the strategy and structure," he says. "You've met everyone, but here's how they fit into the big picture. Jacob's cool under pressure and keeps us all in line. Adam's a master of disguise."

"And Lucifer," Adrian adds, "is our tech genius, almost as good as Blake, and—"

"And nobody's as good as Blake," Lucifer interjects, "but I can dream." His attention focuses on me. "I work with Blake and manage the surveillance efforts, which by the way, include cameras on your parents' work and home."

"How?" I ask.

He motions to Adam. "He can be anyone and get anywhere. You see a homeless man on a corner, it could be Adam. For a big guy, he can be invisible."

Adam picks up his glass and toasts me.

"Just call him the Invisible Man," Savage says. "We do."

"And last but not least," Adrian says, "is Savage. Yes, he's a killer—"

"Was," Savage says. "I did that shit for the government and now I'm free from them and married. Now, I prefer to call myself a reluctant killer."

"And," Adrian says, "a skilled, licensed surgeon."

I blink. "A surgeon?"

"I'm versatile like that," Savage says, eating yet another piece of bread, after eating a basketful and a burger and fries.

"He saved my life," Adam says. "And so did Adrian."

"As you can tell," Lucifer says, "Adam's always trying to get himself killed."

I inhale on that note and the realization that Adrian was with Adam while Adam was "trying to get himself killed" when he saved Adam's life.

"Overseas operations," Adrian supplies, obviously reading my reaction. "We can opt-in or out of those high-risk jobs."

"This seems pretty high risk right here in Texas," I comment, looking around the table. "And here you all are."

"This is family," Jacob says. "This isn't a job. This is us having each others' backs."

Adrian's fingers flex on my leg where his hand has settled, and there's a tic to his jaw. I don't understand this reaction, but then again, maybe I do. He said the Walker team only knows the Adrian of the past two years. Could he think he'll lose them after he testifies and tells all his dirty deeds?

I wonder if he thinks the same of me.

Chapter Thirty-One

PRI

I don't want the sins of my past to torment me for a lifetime, but I don't know how to escape them. Neither does Adrian, I suspect. I squeeze his hand, eager to assure him in any way possible, even silently, that I understand what he's feeling but he doesn't look at me. The waitress chooses that moment to appear with the dessert menus, and right beside me for that matter, the interruption stealing the moment I'd intended with Adrian.

"Brownie sundaes around the table," Savage declares. "We love that shit."

Adam eyes Adrian and Adrian gives him a nod before capturing my hand. "Let's go talk."

I suspect the brownie sundaes are to buy Adrian time for this talk and I give my easy agreement. Adrian stands and takes me with him, leading me toward a glass door. On the other side, the pungent scent of cigars touches my nose. In a quick glance, I decide we're in what appears to be a private, presently closed, cigar lounge with a private entrance, a bar, and heavy leather chairs paired with thick rugs. I sit on a reddish-brown leather couch and Adrian sits on a coffee table made from a tree trunk.

His hands settle on my knees, just beneath my skirt, his touch intimate, warm, *possessive*. I have a brief memory of how hard Logan tried to own me and failed. I'm confused at how easily Adrian does it without trying. "What do you think of the guys?" he asks.

"You were right. Meeting them gave me confidence, but I'm still worried about you being bait."

"Let's talk about that."

I steel myself for wherever he's going. "Why does that sound ominous?"

"I was selfish to get involved with you, Pri."

That's why I think he's pulling away from me and it's right then that I realize how hard I've already fallen for this man. It's only been a chance encounter and a hot night, and already he can stab me in the heart with rejection. "I see," I manage. "I just—we don't need to do this." I try to get up.

He holds my knees and me in place. "I don't think you do. I have never wanted someone to the point that I couldn't see the risks. I put you in the line of fire."

"I was already in the line of fire. You don't need an excuse to cool us off, Adrian. I get it. It's fine."

"Is it? Is it that easy for you to cool us off?"

I blink. "You're confusing me right now."

"Then let me be clear," he says, leaning in closer, the masculine spice of his cologne a wicked play on my senses. "I don't want to let you go and it's too late anyway."

My brows furrow. "Too late?"

"Waters insisted on meeting with you, not Ed. He doesn't communicate with anyone but the top dog. I believe he knows we're together. I believe you're a target because of me."

I suddenly understand why he wasn't touching me outside, in the public eye where our relationship would be in plain view. "I was a target anyway."

"I betrayed him. I earned his trust and betrayed him. He wants me to pay. He'll go after what I care about."

"Just because you sleep with me doesn't mean you care about me." I hold up a hand. "I'm not saying you don't."

"I do," he says, his voice a low rumble, almost a growl. "You *know* I do."

I study his earnest expression and press my hand to his face. "I do know, but you also know that I have my own sins I'm playing to right now. My own dirty side. I'm in this all the way. I'm not scared. So knowing that, now what?"

He captures my hands. "We have options. Number one, Ed could go with me today before he goes into hiding."

"No. I don't trust Ed. His assistant is suddenly on an unexpected vacation, and he's acting off. No. He might turn on you."

"Number two. I could go alone."

"No," I say again. "The DA has to be represented in a firm 'no deal' statement. I'm going with you, so now what?"

"Number three starts with my strategy. I'm visiting Waters to taunt him. He'll bite and he'll force Deleon to come for me and you, on our terms and do so now. We go in there today. We push Waters' buttons. We go home to your place and when the sun goes down, we sneak out and my men handle Deleon."

"And we'll be where?"

"Miles away in a place he'll never find us, just you and me. I'll set up secure communications for you. You can manage the case from a distance."

"I'll make it work, but what if Deleon doesn't come for us?"

"He will," he says, his tone absolute.

"Okay, well let's say he does and all goes well. What's to keep Waters from sending someone else after us?"

"The goal is to capture his men alive and turn at least a few against him. That might force a deal he's not going to take now."

"Will Deleon flip?" I ask hopefully.

"Never. It has to be some of the lessers down the food chain. If that doesn't happen, we'll stay off the grid until the trial, and we'll keep our team close during the trial. But you don't have to do this today."

"Don't you want to be a part of taking down Deleon?"

"I trust the guys and I'm not leaving you. We leave tonight and we do it together."

Chapter Thirty-Two

PRI

I eat the chocolate brownie sundae.

I mean, if I'm going to die soon, macaroni and cheese, chocolate, and ice cream need to be a part of my final days. And Adrian. I need more Adrian. In the process, I end up with a whole lot more Walker Security as well, which is just fine by me. I like these guys, especially as they get focused on planning, and Lucifer pulls out a MacBook to check in with the rest of their team.

By the time me, Adrian, and Adam are back inside the SUV, on our way to the Del Valle detention center where Waters is being held pending trial, I'm feeling ready for our meeting with him. That is until my cellphone rings and the caller ID is my father's number. Just that easily, I'm twisted in knots. I'm pretty sure that alone establishes me as having enough personal baggage to fill a 737's hungry belly. I decline the call and glance at Adrian. "Can you just confirm for me that my parents are safe right now?"

"I'd hear if they weren't. Why?"

"My father just called and while I don't want to talk to him before the Waters' meeting, he *never* calls. It could be about Logan, but I just need to be sure."

He studies me for a probing moment—seeing too much, I suspect—but I really don't have it in me to hide my private demons right now. I'm not sure I'd try with Adrian if I did. "I'm sorry, sweetheart," he says, "but I need you to call him back in case it affects the meeting in some way." He pulls his phone from his pocket. "But I'm also shooting a message to our team to confirm all is well with his security detail."

I inhale an uncomfortably thick breath and wait as he shoots a text to someone. The reply is instant and Adrian looks at me. "The man watching your parents says all clear."

"All right then," I say, "I'll just dial him up and have a little father-daughter chat." I punch in the auto-dial and my father answers on the first ring.

"Pri," he says, his voice deep, distinguished, and you almost know he's a good-looking man without ever seeing him. My father's a stud. All the women think so, including my mother, who seems to manage him in ways no one else could. "I thought for a moment there you were going to blow me off," he adds.

"Why would I do that?"

"We both know we haven't exactly endured the choppy waters we created to find our calmer sea."

"No," I agree. "I suppose we haven't."

"Logan wants you back. He's not the only one. I do, too."

"He wants me back to do damage control."

"I don't know what his agenda is, but it fits mine so that works for me and I do believe it works for our family."

"Why do you want me off the Waters case?"

"I don't," he says without hesitation. "And if I might speak outside our little deal to not talk about business?"

"Yes, please do."

"I want you to stay on it and win and then come on back over here, and bill the hell out of that win."

I can almost believe him since he's talking money, but not quite. "Mom and Logan said you wanted me off the case. Or Mom did. Logan spoke for himself."

"Exactly. Who speaks for me but me?"

"True," I say. "But Logan—"

"Has an agenda. He wants you back here with that ring on your finger. You two were a real power couple."

"If you start down this Logan-loving path again, Dad, this call is over."

"I'm simply stating his motivations. And Mom is worried about you. She was never going to leave town when you might need her, by the way."

I should have known that, I think. My mother is flawed, but in her own way, she loves me. And I love my parents despite all our conflicts. "I'm not coming back."

"Let's have dinner."

In other words, he's unfazed by my decline and setting up negotiations. "Not until after the trial," I say. "And if I lose, what would there be to talk about?"

"You won't lose. You never lose. But after the trial works. We'll do Thanksgiving together and talk about the future. Be careful. It's a different game being on the bad side of the bad guys." Someone speaks to him. "Gotta run. Win big, my girl." He disconnects.

I lower the phone and glance at Adrian. "Nothing interesting. Just him wanting to cash in on me winning this case."

"He wants you to come back to the family biz," he assumes.

"That's never going to happen," I assure him. "But what's interesting is him being at odds with Logan over the Waters case. He says he wants me to stay on it.

Logan wants me off. Somehow Logan made a deal with someone and he's desperate to get me off this case."

"And yet, he went to your father for help?"

"He went to my father about getting me back. My father took his own angle on making that happen. Can Lucifer dig around and see what kind of trouble Logan might be in? There feels like there is more going on with him than what's on the surface."

"I'll have him check him out," he agrees. "And I'll have him look for ties to Waters outside of Whitaker."

"With his client list, I'm sure he'll find some," I warn. "I'm not sure it will be as easy as that to pin down what's really going on. And don't forget to tell him about Ed's assistant suddenly taking an unplanned vacation during Ed's reelection and this trial."

Adrian calls Lucifer and while they talk, I am thinking about that call with my father and the way he twisted my new career, my repenting for my sins, into his money-making opportunity. Unbidden, I drift back into the past, momentarily back to a day when I was still working for my father. I was at lunch in the restaurant on the lower level of the firm's building with my then-friend Susan, a pretty redhead and up-and-coming attorney in the firm.

I sign my credit card slip, and Logan walks in, eyeing me and Susan. I cut my stare, and Susan lowers her voice. "Are you ever going to give him another chance?"

"Never," I say, putting away my card. "I need to get upstairs for a meeting."

"I know he screwed up," she says. "But you haven't been happy since the break-up."

"I wasn't happy before the break-up." I stand up and she does the same.

"I'm headed to the courthouse. Let me know if you want to talk."

"Thanks," I say, but I don't really know her that well and I'm still living in the aftermath of my ex cheating on me with my long-term secretary. I'm not going to talk to her. I'm not in the right headspace to start trusting new people.

I hurry out of the restaurant and ride the elevator upstairs. Once I'm there, I stop by the outrageously fancy break room for a bottle of water, when the news on the big screen television by the seating area catches my attention.

"I repeat," the male newscaster states, "Richard Caine, who was found not guilty of the murder of his business partner just one week ago, has shot and killed his family. He is considered armed and dangerous."

My client, who I thought was innocent. The room spins and I whirl around and start walking. I hurry down the hallway and into my office, slamming the door shut and leaning on the wooden surface. I can barely stand for my trembling legs. My purse falls from my arm and tears burst from me as I sink to the ground. "I'm done," I whisper. "I'm done with this job."

"Pri."

At Adrian's voice, I snap back to the present. "Lucifer wants to talk to you."

I nod and accept his phone, eager to help, that memory spurring my need for action, my determination to make a difference in the right ways, no matter the cost to me. I end up talking to Lucifer for a few minutes, helping him with what he might dig for with Logan and Ed. We disconnect as we reach the security post for the prison and it's not long before Adam pulls us into a parking spot, even less before

Adrian and I exit the vehicle and he turns me to face him.

His hand slides under my hair to my neck and he tilts my face to his. "You don't have to do this."

"And yet, I do. I really do, Adrian. And I want to. Besides, I'm going to face him in court and I'm going to *destroy* him. Better I warm up here and we catch Deleon."

He studies me, his gaze probing, and I don't know what he's looking for, but I know what he finds.

It's not fear. It's determination. And certainty. This is where I belong, and I belong here with him.

Chapter Thirty-Three

ADRIAN

The past...

There are twelve of us, all in Devil jackets around the club table, a devil that matches the one on my arm carved in the wood. Waters, the King Devil, is at the head of the table, ruler of this land, in this world. He's forty-two, brutally vicious, sporting a dark beard with hints of gray, but doesn't drink or do drugs. He just peddles drugs, weapons, and women, while pumping iron, and adding new tattoos.

And after two years of hell undercover, I'm now one of his two most trusted men.

I'm to his right. Jose Deleon is to his left. I'm his strategist. Deleon is his fixer, a man who kills for sport.

"We have a new opportunity," Waters says to the table. "Our Dark Knight has a new opportunity. Lots of money and women."

After two years undercover for the Feds with this shit show, the Dark Knight, as Waters calls him, is the only reason I haven't taken them all down for a deluge of crimes, including murder. We know who he is— John Jacobs, the CEO of Mega, the first real competitor to Facebook—but he remains untouchable.

He uses Waters for cover. And John Jacobs is my mission, even beyond Waters.

The door burst open and Devon, one of our newer members, appears holding Sheila, a pretty blonde who runs around with no clothes kissing the King Devil's ass, and anything else he wants, daily. "She's been stealing from you, King Devil. I found her digging around in your office."

Sheila starts screaming. "I wanted to surprise you with a gift. I was looking for ideas. I swear. It's almost your birthday."

Which is true, but I glance at Waters and he's not buying it. Evil hums from him. Deleon meets my stare and smirks with amusement. He's already enjoying her certain demise. My fingers curl by my sides and I know, I know, this is one of those times I'll be forced to walk away, forced to endure what I cannot stop.

Waters stands up. "I need to be someplace. She's probably talking to the cops. Have fun with her, punish her, but don't kill her until I talk to her." He glances at me and then Deleon, motioning us toward the door. We both stand and follow him and already Sheila is in a corner, out of view, with three men in front of her.

I grimace, adrenaline surging through me, fighting the clawing need to save her and shoot every motherfucker in this place. But I can't. There are women being held captive in camps that will be moved and lost if I blow my cover and crimes that will go unanswered. Sheila will end up dead and I won't be able to connect it to Waters.

I keep walking and shut the fucking door on a woman in need, wondering what will be left of me when this is over. I wonder if I'll still recognize myself. Who am I kidding? I already don't.

Once we're in the main clubhouse, Waters motions us to the porch. We step outside and his phone rings. He answers the call and steps away from us.

"You don't like to see the women touched," Deleon comments, leaning on the railing, elbows on the wooden ledge.

I lean on the same ledge, my back to the wood, and cross my arms over my chest. "I don't see you partaking in the festivities yourself."

"Nah," he says. "You know me, man. I like my women soft and moaning." He turns around to face the same direction as me. "King Devil knows I'll kill 'em, but I don't want to fuck 'em. I'm about business and money. We're alike in that."

He thinks we're alike and he's not wrong. He's a killer and before this is over, I predict I will be, too. And he's the one who will be dead.

The present...

Waters attorney finally arrives over an hour late, which I suspect has something to do with him finding out I'm present.

Once we're in the main hallway leading to the secure room where Waters has been taken, I stop Pri just beyond the guard's reach. And holy hell, she's beautiful, the kind of beauty Waters will get off on in all the wrong ways. "He's a monster. He will try to get under your skin."

"I know his type," she says, "too well."

"Emotions are corruptible tools to use for manipulation."

"So my father preached to m from the day I could walk."

"Waters will tell you how fuckable you are. How I'm using you. He'll say some crass things, like asking you how good I am with my tongue. He loves that line."

She blanches. "I—ah—thanks for the warning. And for the record, between us, very good."

My lips curve. "Is that right?"

"Yes. It is. Can we get this over with?"

I study her a moment, looking for any sign she doesn't want to do this, but I find only determination. "Yes. Let's get this over with." I motion her forward and we close the space between us and the guard. The man in uniform, with a belly that says he loves beer, buzzes the door and I hold it open for Pri. With her head held high, her body language confident and fearless, she enters the room with me quickly following. Waters, dressed in a black-striped prison uniform, sits behind the only furniture in the small concrete room—a basic table. Beside him is Daniel White, his attorney, a lanky man in a suit, wearing thick-rimmed glasses. Waters' eyes meet mine and cut like hot steel, the devil himself in the depths of his green eyes. His lips quirk with amusement.

White pushes to his feet and eyes me, shifting to Pri, as he demands, "Who's this?" as if I'm not able to speak myself and he doesn't already know anyway.

"That, Daniel," Waters replies, "is the prosecution's star witness, Adrian Mack."

Daniel smirks. "The star witness that committed crimes you can testify to." He offers Pri a gloating look. "Maybe we should have him on our three for one list."

Pri steps to the opposite side of the table, across from Daniel, meeting him head on. "I don't need a list. No deal."

Waters' eyes fix on her as I step in front of him. He glances at me. "Nice piece of pussy. I see why you're fucking her. She can get you off and keep you out of jail."

I lean on the table and look him in the eyes. "Maybe if you get Daniel off in the back room, he'll do the same for you."

His lips curve. "I'd rather lick Priscilla. Or is it Pri?" He leans closer. "No one is as good at being bad as you were, Adrian Mack, if they're not really bad."

"And yet, I didn't kill you."

"You didn't *want* to kill me."

He's wrong. I wanted it like I have never wanted anything in my life.

Daniel clears his throat and sets a piece of paper on the table. "The list."

Pri waves it off. "Irrelevant. I said no deal."

"Then I'll talk to the DA," Daniel counters.

"Ed signed off on this," Pri says, cool and confident, unfazed by Waters, at least on the surface, "and he's now taken an extended vacation."

"Good," Waters says. "Vacations help people relax and let their guard down."

"If Ed is really on board with the no deal strategy," Daniel says, "he won't mind if we send the list to the press, I assume?"

"Not at all," Pri states, her eyes daring to meet Waters'. "And he and I will both tell the press all the reasons you won't go free. We're done." She looks at me and in silent agreement, we turn for the door.

I've just reached for the handle when Waters says, "It's always hard to say goodbye to the pretty ones, don't you think, Adrian?"

It's a threat against Pri, and despite expecting as much, it jars me. I inhale, all but radiating with my need to go over that table and destroy him, but once again, one last time with this monster, I hold back. I don't, however, walk away. I know him and when he's angry he acts quickly, or rather, he orders Deleon to act quickly. I use this moment and that knowledge as a chance to push him a little harder, to make sure he wants me dead tonight.

I walk to the table, press my hands to the top again, get in his face and say, "It's over for you," I goad, trying to get him to threaten me on camera. "I'm the end for you."

"You're overly confident, Adrian. The end is near, but it won't be the end you write. It'll be the end I write. The one I'm writing in my head this very moment."

"In handcuffs, a striped suit, and about to go back to jail. I could have justified killing you twenty times over and if I believed you could hurt me, I would have. But I don't. You're pathetic, barely a man, one who had to hide behind his Dark Knight. I wanted you here. Learning what it's like to be someone's little bitch. And you will, many times over." I push off the table and walk to the door, opening it and urging Pri into the hallway.

We leave Waters behind, but this isn't the end of my story with Waters.

If we play our cards right, it will be the end of Deleon.

Chapter Thirty-Four

PRI

Once we're in the SUV, Adrian kisses me. "You did good, sweetheart. You okay?"

"Yes. I just want that monster to go down."

"And he will," he vows. "I really am the end of him." He strokes my hair and leans forward to talk to Adam, who sets us in motion.

I'm not listening to their conversation, though. I'm thinking of the interaction between Adrian and Waters. He asked if I'm okay. I know now, that deep beneath his surface, beneath the jokes and good nature, is a man tormented with deep scars. He calls himself dirty because he feels dirty, but I'm the one who's dirty. I'm the one who helped people like Waters for money and accolades. He did what he did for the greater good, and I'm going to make sure he remembers that and it won't be easy. Not when the press and the defense team will try to paint him as dirty as he feels.

Adam drops me and Adrian off at my office building, a necessity to ensure that he's not followed back to the rental where the team is working. "Let's walk to your place," Adrian says. "And quickly, before you get cornered by someone exiting the offices."

"You're making sure Deleon sees you."

"He's seen me already," he says. "Waters made that clear. Right now, I'm taunting him, telling him I'm not afraid of him." He grabs my briefcase. "I'll carry this. Do you need your flats?" He pulls them from my bag.

"Yes," I say. "Thank you. And your arm." I hold onto him, changing my shoes, struck by how comfortable I already am with Adrian, and I think that matters. It feels like a natural trust level I instinctively have for him. And somehow, he's exciting and comfortable.

I slip my heels into my bag hanging at his side.

"You're back to being very short," he comments, "but you handled yourself like you were ten feet tall in there with Waters today." He motions me forward and we start walking.

"I have a zone I get into when I'm with those monsters." I glance over at him. "I'm sure you get it."

He cuts his stare, and looks skyward a moment. "I do."

"I can't imagine what it was like being on duty, living undercover for two years," I say, trying to remind him that he was on duty, doing a job, and what that job forced him to do isn't what defines him.

His answer is slow, and for a few beats I think he won't answer at all. "You have to become the character you're playing," he says softly, but adds nothing more.

I decide not to push him, not now, and instead, change the subject. "Obviously Waters' people were watching us and we didn't know it. Is that a concern? Maybe they already know where your team is holing up."

"I suspect Deleon had a man watching you," he says, "just in case he had to target you, which probably means the coffee shop, which led to me. I knew approaching you was a risk, but they didn't have any real recon, or we'd know." He slides his arm around me. "I promise. The team is in control."

I trust his team, I do, but this is all unsettling, and how can it not be? People are dead, murdered for crossing Waters and we have both crossed Waters. For now, though, we approach my front door, and I focus on what's in front of me. "Is this really a good idea?" I ask. "I mean can't Deleon just show up now?"

"Savage and Jacob are already inside," he says, and I remember overhearing him and Adam talking about this while my head was still in that room with Waters. "Adam will join them after dark," he adds. "Dexter is still with Ed. Once we leave, anyone watching will still see them moving about the house. At nightfall, we'll leave."

I glance at my watch. "Somehow it's six-thirty already now. That's not going to be long."

"Just enough time for you to pack and for us to order food. Go through the motions and punch in your code."

"Right," I say, doing as instructed and punching in my code.

Adrian opens the door and I enter, turning to face him, the sound of Savage's voice lifting from the kitchen. "Your team being here is comforting," I say, setting my purse down. "But what's not," I add, "is the way they can enter at will despite my security system."

"Technology can be deceivingly comforting," Adrian says, locking up again and setting my briefcase next to my purse. "But you have to remember the average criminal can't do what Lucifer can." He steps close, big and warm and hard, all things I find extremely wonderful right now.

"You're so calm," I comment, "like we didn't just invite a killer to come after us."

"We won't be here when they come," he says. "We're safe right now. I promise. You need to pack, though, so we're ready to leave when the guys give the heads up."

"Pack for how long?"

"Possibly until the trial but we need to stay light, a small duffle on top of your purse and briefcase is all we can risk right now. We're going over your fence in the dark. If we have to stay in hiding we'll go shopping. Back to food. Pizza is easy. You want to just get pizza again?"

I'm still digesting the part where we're going over the fence but manage a nod. "Yes. Good." I grab my purse again, really needing my gun nearby when I walk through the house, despite all the Walker men present. "I'll hurry."

I twist out of his reach and hurry down the hallway. My heart is racing and my hand is in my purse, on my weapon, when I flip on my bedroom light, relieved when there's no monster waiting on me. I follow the same process in the bathroom and closet. When all is clear, I change into jeans, a T-shirt, and boots before filling a small bag. I don't end up with much and I don't even care. Suddenly, the reality of what we did today hits me like a ten-ton truck and I sink onto my vanity chair, hands on my face, willing my mind to calm.

There's a shift in the air and I swear I feel Adrian even before he appears, and then he's on his knee in front of me. "You okay?"

I drop my hands and cover his with mine. "I am. I just—I don't know what I'm doing anymore. I want to do good, but this is insanity. The level of corruption, the politics, the danger."

"Waters is a once in a lifetime kind of case, Pri."

"But he lets me see the layers of corruption. He lets me see that people aren't always what they seem. I think I thought that working for the prosecution insulated me from such things." I study him a moment, this complicated man, I've only just met, but who I believe understands me more than people I've known most of my life. "I know I want to make a difference in the world," I say, "but I don't know if this is how I want to do it. I mean, look at you. You left the Feds after Waters. You had to have felt the same kind of internal conflict."

It's a statement but also a question.

"I think you already know that's a long and complicated story but yes, I left. I was done after Waters."

"I think I might be, too."

"Don't make that decision now. Decide after you put him in jail and if you leave, leave on your terms."

"Not over a fence in the dark?" I joke, giving a choked laugh.

"Not unless you have pizza in your belly." He winks and stands, taking me with him, caressing my hair behind my ear, his touch sending a shiver over my skin. "A few more hours and we'll be out of here, safe, and by the time we wake up tomorrow, at least part of this story is over."

And yet, my gut tells me the nightmare has just begun.

Chapter Thirty-Five

ADRIAN

Pri's on edge and I understand why. Being under fire in the courtroom is her thing. Being under fire outside the courtroom is mine.

Once the pizza arrives and she's with me, Savage, and Jacob at the island, eating, she seems to relax, at least a small amount, laughing as Savage and I banter. Unfortunately, the escape from reality that laughter represents is short-lived. Savage's phone buzzes and he answers the call, listens, and says, "We're moving." He disconnects and focuses on me. "A storm is rolling in. Lucifer thinks you need to move now before it hits and makes it harder to make the change."

"Will a storm stop Deleon from attacking?" Pri asks.

"The opposite," I say, standing up. "A muddy, wet house hides evidence."

"Right," she says. "I, of all people, know that."

I stand and motion to her phone where it rests on the table. "Leave it. We can't let them use it to track us. We'll get you set-up with a new one soon."

She hesitates but nods her approval.

Five minutes later, I'm helping Pri over a fence, thunder rumbling above, the scent of rain in the air, the humidity downright suffocating. Once we're on the ground in the yard next door, we do the same two more times, and exit to another neighborhood street. A quick scan of the area reads safe and I spy the white Ford F150 pickup I'm looking for—a truck our team chose for the simple fact that it's a Texas favorite, in every other driveway, thus it doesn't stand out.

"That's us," I say, motioning to the truck and then helping her inside the passenger side. "Lock it," I order, scanning the area one last time, as I round the truck bed and quickly find my way to the driver's door. About the time I climb behind the wheel, joining Pri and locking up, the first drop of rain hits the window.

"We're in for a wet ride," I say, cranking the engine and wasting no time setting us in motion.

"Where are we going?" she asks. "I don't think you ever told me."

"A cabin out by the lake my father left me for just such an occasion. It's deeded under a fake name and meant to be an escape if he needed it, and now, I need it." I'm already pulling us out of the neighborhood, and the edge of my mood begins to settle, the adrenaline rush of getting her out of her place safely with it. "Snuggle in and get cozy, sweetheart," I say. "We have an hour-long drive."

She scoots over beside me and rests her head on my arm, glancing up at me. "Is this okay?"

I wait for some kind of internal push-back, some rejection of my growing bond with Pri, but it's not there. Something inside me is changing, and it's all about her. "Yes," I say. "Perfect."

She's perfect, I think a while later when the rain is steady and so is her breathing. Too perfect for me and it guts me to know that it won't be long until she agrees.

Chapter Thirty-Six

ADRIAN

When we hit the gravel road not far from the cabin, with rain pounding the windows, Pri bustles to life, sitting up with a jolt. "What's happening?"

"Bad roads," I say. "Easy, sweetheart. All is well."

Her shoulders roll forward. "Thank God. How long was I out?"

"Most of the drive. We're about to arrive now."

She presses her hands to her face and then her legs, as if she's trying to get her circulation pumping. "I can't believe I slept that hard."

"We did sleep on the couch last night and it's been an intense day."

"True," I say. "Very true." She scans the woods around us. "Good thing we ate before we left."

"We have some supplies, but nothing fancy. I have chocolate and booze, though."

"Well then," she laughs, "we're living like kings." She groans. "Why'd I have to bring *him* into this?"

"At least you said kings and not devils, but Waters is all over our lives right now, sweetheart." I point ahead as the wood cabin comes into view and then maneuver us close to the front door and porch. "It's not the Ritz, but it's cozy." I kill the engine. "Hang tight and I'll help you avoid the mud." I open the door and rush out into the cold rain, drenched in about ten seconds, but I plug onward.

Pri opens her door and I scoop her up and out of the rain quickly before carrying her up the steps to set her on the porch. "I'll grab our bags," I say, rushing back out into the rain and returning with her bag, and shortly after, another three the guys packed for us.

"You're dripping," Pri worries as I unlock the cabin door and flip the switch controlling the lamp in the living room.

"I have clothes to change into and we have power which in this case means power to run the air conditioner we'll need when the rain passes. My father pre-paid in cash for the power for several years in advance." I push open the door and motion her inside, quickly joining her. She scans the plastic-covered couches, and fireplace, while I toss the bags to the floor by the door. "Like I said," locking up and kneeling by my bag to pull out a change of clothes. "It's not the Ritz."

"I don't need the Ritz," she says. "I just want to stay alive."

"The back and sides of the house are booby-trapped by the way. If anyone comes at us beyond the front door, they're in for a painful surprise. My father knew how to cover his bases. You can feel safe here."

"Booby traps," she murmurs. "I don't know what to say to that."

"We won't need them," I assure her, pulling off my wet T-shirt and replacing it with a dry one, then standing with a dry pair of jeans in my hands. "Kitchen," I say, pointing to the right where a brown table sits. "One bedroom and bathroom. I'm going to go check those rooms."

"I'll uncover the furniture," she offers, and I nod, heading to the back, checking things out, and then drying off before changing pants.

Once I've returned to the main room, I find the basic brown couches exposed and Pri kneeling by the bags. She holds up a candy bag. "We have plenty of M & M's, I see."

"Dessert and superpower food."

She laughs and pulls out a bag of Cheetos. "Also superpower food."

"You know it," I assure her. "Now we just need whiskey. See if there's any soda in those bags, will you? I have frozen and canned foods, if we need them to get by but Savage packed us some extras." I walk into the dusty-ass kitchen, and find an equally dusty-ass bottle of whiskey, a couple bottles of water, and two plastic Solo cups, before returning to the living area.

Pri stands up, holding the candy, and displaying a small bottle the size of a salt shaker between her index finger and thumb. "It's called Sweet Tea Mio, one of those flavor additives for water, and there's a note from Savage that reads, 'Water, Mio, whiskey. Thank me later.'"

"Savage knows his whiskey, so let's give it a try." I motion to the living room and we settle onto the couch. Pri's already removed the plastic from the basic wooden coffee table and we set our haul on top. "No cable," I say, filling our glasses with whiskey and water, while Pri adds the Mio. "But we have computers."

"What about the internet?"

"Lucifer will give you a secure line. I have a new phone for you, and Lucifer will forward your calls to it." I hand her a glass and lift mine. "Shall we try it?"

"I'm all in," she says, and we both take a sip, the sweet mix of tea and whiskey a surprisingly good combination.

"I like it," Pri says. "And I don't even really like whiskey." She takes another sip and leans back onto the couch cushion, facing me. "Tell me about your father."

I lean into the couch facing her. "He was a good man, a proud man. A skilled agent. He made me want to be a better man."

"And mine made me want to bill the highest dollars. I let the money go to my head and I'm not proud of that."

"Because that's the bar your father set for you to be successful. Hell, I like money, too. I made more money with Walker during my first year with them than I would have my entire career in the FBI. And I got to do good things."

"That much money?"

"Yes," I say. "But I did go overseas."

"And did what there?"

"Rescued a foreign diplomat's daughter, and captured a terrorist, among other things. Pretty much it's the rite of passage for Walker. We all go, make our money, and decide when we've had enough."

"Is it a requirement?" she asks, reaching for her drink as if she suddenly needs it.

"It's not. Nothing but honesty and integrity are requirements at Walker and they share the profit with us all anyway, even stateside."

She sips her drink and sets it back down before scooting closer to me, her hand on my leg, her touch tempting me already. "Tell me something," she says.

"All right," I say, steeling myself for a question I'm not willing to answer now.

"Wasn't Savage some sort of assassin?"

"A mercenary and yes, an assassin."

"And he's been with Walker how long?" she asks.

"A few years longer than me," I say cautiously. "Why?"

"If he's with Walker, why do you believe Walker will turn their backs on you after you testify? Because you do. I know you do."

I cup her face, regret in my answer, I don't hide. "The same reason I know you will. I had to play the role. I had to let people get hurt."

Her hand covers my hand on her face. "I let people get hurt by helping bad people stay out of jail. I'm not going to turn my back on you. I'm not. Try me."

"I can't do that, not without the immunity deal."

She pulls back to look at me, a stab of pain in her stare. "Do you think I'd use what you tell me tonight against you? Do you really think that of me?"

"I think you're a good person, even if you question that. But you have a legal obligation to expose what you know. I'm not going to compromise you in that way."

"You have immunity."

"For reasonable justified actions. I went beyond that, Pri."

"Do you think guilt is controlling you, even effecting your judgment?"

"No." I tangle fingers into her tousled dark hair and pull her mouth to mine. "We aren't having this conversation right now. I'm not ready for you to hate me."

"I'm not going to hate you."

"And yet, you will." I brush my lips over hers and whisper, "You're going to be the death of me, woman."

"Maybe I'll save you," she answers. "Maybe we'll save each other."

Or maybe I'll destroy you, I think, but still my mouth closes down on her mouth, and the instant our tongues collide, there's a shift in the air, hunger spiking between us, demanding and ferocious in its need. The sweet taste of her is now my new obsession and I can't get enough.

We're all over each other, tugging at clothes, shifting and moving. There is no slow burn, not this night, not this time. There is just this sense of standing on the edge of a world that is no longer round, and we are falling, crashing, into each other. When we're naked, and she's straddling me, she's not shy about touching me. I hold her up, anchor her, and she's holding my cock, pressing it inside all that warm perfect heat of her sex.

She slides down me, pressing against me, settling low, taking all of me and it's fucking perfection. She's perfection: her ivory skin, her high breasts, her nipples puckered and pink.

Her gaze lands on my devil tattoo and I go still, waiting for her realization of just how deep I was inside the Devils, how a part of them I was, and always will be. Her hand covers the ink and her gaze lifts to mine. "You will always be a devil."

And there it is. Her realization. "I've been telling you that."

"You're too busy denying that part of yourself to survive it."

"What does that mean?"

"It means embrace and use it."

I catch her hair with my fingers again, and this time I'm not gentle. She just won't listen. She won't stop pushing me to a place she thinks she needs to go but doesn't. She really fucking doesn't. "You don't know what you're suggesting."

"Show me," she says. "Let that part of you fuck me right here, right now."

My rejection is instant. "You will never know that part of me."

"Then I'll never know you."

"I don't want to hurt you, Pri, and I will. I will never be the man who deserves you. You need to know that."

"What if you already are?"

"I was him, before Waters, but I'm not the same man I was then. I won't be him again."

"I don't know that man. I know this one. I want to know more, the good, the bad, and the dirty. I can handle it."

Until she can't, I think, but I want her to, so fucking much. My fingers relax in her hair, my hand cupping her head. And I feel her in ways I have never felt another woman and she's burning me alive.

I know I should stop this, stop *us,* let her go, but right now, it feels like losing her would be cutting off a part of my own body which is crazy—I've only just met her. I thought I was fine with dying on those missions for Walker. Now I want to live. And part of me wants to punish her for making us both want what we can't have. This will end. We will end.

My mouth slants over hers, and I'm kissing her, drinking her in and I don't hold back and neither does she. Our tongues connect, stroke, battle. I can taste her demand. She wants what I won't give. She wants me to fuck her like the devil I am. And I could. I could so easily demand everything and expect her to give it to me. I could take her in ways she's never been taken. And then she'd prove me right. She'd prove she can't handle that part of me.

I tug her shirt over her head and shove her bra down, my fingers teasing her nipple. Her teeth scrape her bottom lip and when I cover her breast with my hand, she covers my hand. Almost as if she's holding onto control. I lean in and kiss her, and she pants into my mouth, and I revel in the fact that her control is already gone. I nip her bottom lip, lapping at the offended skin, my fingers still tangled into her hair again.

I kiss her hard and fast, and mold every soft curve she owns against me, one hand scooping her perfect little ass. My lips linger just above hers, and there is no denying the deep ache Pri stirs in me, unfamiliar and somehow intrusive, and yet still additive. Too addictive for me to let her go.

She leans into me, her body submissive, a plea for me to go further, to show her everything there is to show. She wants to be pushed, to escape with me, but I hold back. I'm too close to the edge, too close to a part of me that may not be gentle. Tonight, our sins will stay our own. They will not be mine.

Angry at her for trusting so easily, angry at myself for where I almost went with Pri, tormented by how easy it was, I pull my mouth from hers. Her hand presses to my face and she whispers, "I'd tell you to stop deciding for me, but I think I owe you the same."

It's exactly what I need to hear and there's an instant spike between us. The burn is provocative, almost dark and volatile, pulsing between us, a living thing, a band wrapping us together. We explode into passion, our clothes no longer on our bodies, our passion no longer contained. I roll her to her back, kissing her, driving into her, until she trembles in my arms, her sex clenching around me. She drags me with her, my body quaking, the world fading.

I end up on my back with her snuggled to my side, the sweet scent of floral perfume and warrior princess teasing my nostrils. And she is a warrior. She proved that today. And I dare to think that maybe, just maybe, we can battle the devil and our own demons, and together, we'll win.

LISA RENEE JONES

Chapter Thirty-Seven

ADRIAN

Something wakes me up from where we sleep on the couch.

I lay there, Pri naked and still snuggled into my side, the dim light of the lamp casting shadows on the ceiling, unease clawing at me. I reach above my head and turn out the light. Seconds turn into a full minute and there's a flicker of light outside the window, somewhere in the not too far distance. *Holy fuck.* We should be safe here. I wasn't followed. I know I wasn't followed.

Focused on action now, I grab my phone and text "911" to Lucifer, and shift Pri, leaning in to whisper. "We have trouble. Get dressed quietly."

She is up instantly, and even in the darkness, I can see the fear etched on her pretty face, but I can't comfort her now. I dress quickly, my gun at the back of my pants, a blade in my each of my boots. Another in my hand.

Footsteps stomp up the stairs. "Adrian, it's Pitt."

I flip on the light, and Pri whispers. "How can he be here? How does he know you're here and oh God. Is your team—"

"No," I say, grabbing my phone and dialing Lucifer.

He answers immediately with, "Savage is on his way," and I feel relief about the backup and the team's safety. "We're silent here," he adds. "What's happening?" I glance at Pri and say, "They're fine," before turning my attention back to the call. "Agent Pitt is here. Find out why."

"I thought you said no one knows that place?" he asks.

Another knock at the door. "Adrian! Are you there, man?"

I focus on answering Lucifer. "They don't. This is nothing good. I'm taking us underground. You know what to do."

"Copy that," he says, and I hang up, sliding my phone into my pocket. "Where's your gun?"

"Purse," she says, "by the door."

"I'll grab it for you and then I need you to go to the hallway behind the living room. I don't want you near a window. Don't leave the house without me. There are explosives back there."

"Okay," she says. "My God. Okay."

I'm already walking, snatching her purse and handing it to her. "Go," I mouth, flipping on the porch light and glancing out the window. Pitt is alone, at least for now.

My knife flips to my palm, out of sight, and I unbolt the door and open it. He has on a rain jacket, his hands free and visible. "What the fuck are you doing here?"

"I got a message to meet you here. Could you have picked a crappier night, my man? But damn, you're a sight for sore eyes."

"I didn't leave you a message."

His eyes narrow. "Fuck. You didn't, did you?"

"No. I didn't. So what the hell is going on?"

"Can I get off this porch where I'm a target?"

I back up and let him enter for no reason other than I want the door shut again. He doesn't have a chance one-on-one with me. He steps forward and then jerks abruptly, his eyes going wild, a choking sound gurgling from him. His body falls forward, and Deleon is standing there. "Hello, friend," he greets.

THE END...FOR NOW

Adrian's trilogy continues very soon in **WHEN HE'S BAD**! Be sure you've pre-ordered so you're one of the first to find out what happens when Adrian is faced with the devils of his past head-on.

PRE-ORDER HERE:

https://www.lisareneejones.com/walker-security-adrians-trilogy.html

If you loved the other Walker Security men, check out the other series from that world: Tall, Dark, and Deadly, Walker Security, and Savage's own four-book series—the finale in his series is releasing early next year!

Don't forget, if you want to be the first to know about upcoming books, giveaways, sales and any other exciting news I have to share please be sure you're signed up for my newsletter! As an added bonus everyone receives a free ebook when they sign-up!

http://lisareneejones.com/newsletter-sign-up/

The Brilliance Trilogy

It all started with a note, just a simple note hand written by a woman I didn't know, never even met. But in that note is perhaps every answer to every question I've ever had in my life. And because of that note, I look for her, but find him. I'm drawn to his passion, his talent, a darkness in him that somehow becomes my light, my life. Kace August is rich, powerful, a rock star of violins, a man who is all tattoos, leather, good looks and talent. He has a wickedly sweet ability to play the violin, seducing audiences worldwide. Now, he's seducing me. I know he has secrets. I don't care. Because you see, I have secrets, too.

I'm not Aria Alard, as he believes. I'm Aria Stradivari, daughter to Alessandro Stradivari, a musician born from the same blood as the man who created the famous Stradivarius violin. I am as rare as the mere 650 instruments my ancestors created. Instruments worth millions. 650 masterpieces, the brilliance unmatched. 650 reasons to kill. 650 reasons to hide. One reason not to: him.

FIND OUT MORE ABOUT THE BRILLIANCE TRILOGY HERE:

https://www.lisareneejones.com/brilliance-trilogy.html

***

GET BOOK ONE, A RECKLESS NOTE, FREE EXCLUSIVELY HERE:

https://claims.prolificworks.com/free/sYEuj2pM

Excerpt from
the Savage series

He's here.

Rick is standing right in front of me, bigger than life, and so damn him, in that him kind of way that I couldn't explain if I tried. He steps closer and I drop my bag on the counter. He will hurt me again, I remind myself, but like that first night, I don't seem to care.

I step toward him, but he's already there, already here, right here with me. I can't even believe it's true. He folds me close, his big, hard body absorbing mine. His fingers tangle in my hair, his lips slanting over my lips. And then he's kissing me, kissing me with the intensity of a man who can't breathe without me. And I can't breathe without him. I haven't drawn a real breath since he sent me that letter.

My arms slide under his tuxedo jacket, wrapping his body, muscles flexing under my touch. The heat of his body burning into mine, sunshine warming the ice in my heart he created when he left. And that's what scares me. Just this quickly, I'm consumed by him, the princess and the warrior, as he used to call us. My man. My hero. And those are dangerous things for me to feel, so very dangerous. Because they're not real. He showed me that they aren't real.

"This means nothing," I say, tearing my mouth from his, my hand planting on the hard wall of his chest. "This is sex. Just sex. This changes nothing."

"Baby, we were never just sex."

"We are not the us of the past," I say, grabbing his lapel. "I just need—you owe me this. You owe me a proper—"

"Everything," he says. "In ways you don't understand, but, baby, you will. I promise you, you will."

I don't try to understand that statement and I really don't get the chance. His mouth is back on my mouth.

The very idea of forever with this man is one part perfect, another part absolute pain. Because there is no forever with this man. But he doesn't give me time to object to a fantasy I'll never own, that I'm not sure I want to try and own again. I don't need forever. I need right now. I need him. I sink back into the kiss and he's ravenous. Claiming me. Taking me. Kissing the hell out of me and God, I love it. God, I need it. I need *him*.

FIND OUT MORE ABOUT THE SAVAGE SERIES HERE:

https://www.lisareneejones.com/savage-series.html

The Lilah Love series

As an FBI profiler, it's Lilah Love's job to think like a killer. And she is very good at her job. When a series of murders surface—the victims all stripped naked and shot in the head—Lilah's instincts tell her it's the work of an assassin, not a serial killer. But when the case takes her back to her hometown in the Hamptons and a mysterious but unmistakable connection to her own life, all her assumptions are shaken to the core.

Thrust into a troubled past she's tried to shut the door on, Lilah's back in the town where her father is mayor, her brother is police chief, and she has an intimate history with the local crime lord's son, Kane Mendez. The two share a devastating secret, and only Kane understands Lilah's own darkest impulses. As more corpses surface, so does a series of anonymous notes to Lilah, threatening to expose her. Is the killer someone in her own circle? And is she the next target?

FIND OUT MORE ABOUT THE LILAH LOVE SERIES HERE:

https://www.lisareneejonesthrillers.com/the-lilah-love-series.html

Also by Lisa Renee Jones

THE INSIDE OUT SERIES

If I Were You
Being Me
Revealing Us
*His Secrets**
Rebecca's Lost Journals
*The Master Undone**
*My Hunger**
No In Between
*My Control**
I Belong to You
*All of Me**

THE SECRET LIFE OF AMY BENSEN

Escaping Reality
Infinite Possibilities
Forsaken
*Unbroken**

CARELESS WHISPERS

Denial
Demand
Surrender

WHITE LIES

Provocative
Shameless

TALL, DARK & DEADLY

Hot Secrets
Dangerous Secrets
Beneath the Secrets

WALKER SECURITY

Deep Under
Pulled Under
Falling Under

LILAH LOVE

Murder Notes
Murder Girl
Love Me Dead
Love Kills
Bloody Vows (January 2021)
Bloody Love (June 2021)

DIRTY RICH

Dirty Rich One Night Stand
Dirty Rich Cinderella Story
Dirty Rich Obsession
Dirty Rich Betrayal
Dirty Rich Cinderella Story: Ever After
Dirty Rich One Night Stand: Two Years Later
Dirty Rich Obsession: All Mine
Dirty Rich Secrets
Dirty Rich Betrayal: Love Me Forever

THE FILTHY TRILOGY

The Bastard
The Princess

The Empire

THE NAKED TRILOGY

One Man
One Woman
Two Together

THE SAVAGE SERIES

Savage Hunger
Savage Burn
Savage Love
Savage Ending

THE BRILLIANCE TRILOGY

A Reckless Note
A Wicked Song
A Sinful Encore

ADRIAN'S TRILOGY

When He's Dirty
When He's Bad (December 2020)
When He's Wild (March 2021)

*eBook only

About the Lisa Renee Jones

New York Times and USA Today bestselling author Lisa Renee Jones writes dark, edgy fiction to include the highly acclaimed INSIDE OUT series and the upcoming, crime thriller The Poet. Suzanne Todd (producer of Alice in Wonderland and Bad Mom's) on the INSIDE OUT series: Lisa has created a beautiful, complicated, and sensual world that is filled with intrigue and suspense.

Prior to publishing Lisa owned a multi-state staffing agency that was recognized many times by The Austin Business Journal and also praised by the Dallas Women's Magazine. In 1998 Lisa was listed as the #7 growing women owned business in Entrepreneur Magazine. She lives in Colorado with her husband, a cat that talks too much, and a Golden Retriever who is afraid of trash bags.

Lisa loves to hear from her readers. You can reach her at lisareneejones.com and she is active on Twitter and Facebook daily.

CPSIA information can be obtained
at www.ICGtesting.com
Printed in the USA
LVHW030852271220
675096LV00006B/896

9 798552 322275